State

LILA ROSE

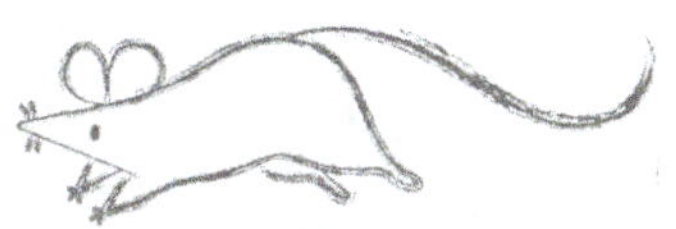

Some people say you can fall for someone at first sight.
I think they're f*cked in the head… until I see her
across the room.

Courtney Anthony has walked into the wrong
clubhouse.
As soon as I spot her, I know what I want.
And what I want most is her.

It's time to see how State meets his old lady.

AUTHOR'S NOTE

This novella is from when State and Courtney first meet and how they come to be a happily married couple.

CHAPTER ONE

State

As I stood next to Country, the president of the MC I was second in command to, I nodded toward the door. "Your woman's here."

Country looked in that direction. But I didn't miss the quick glance at Dusty, a club girl he was fighting his feelings for, thinking she was too young. "Isla said she was bringin' a friend."

I glanced back since I hadn't noticed his woman's friend, and then like an idiot, I did a double take. "Fuck me," I rumbled out low. My damn fantasy just walked into the room.

From first sight, I wanted her.

I wanted my hands in her long, wavy light-brown

hair while I tugged her head back to have her gaze on me and me alone.

She was short, and fuck, it was cute on her.

Her body was… yeah…. My cock jerked and my hands twitched as I shifted on my feet. My body already wanted to be close enough for a touch, a taste.

Country chuckled until I elbowed him in the gut, and he clipped, "Dickhead."

"Introduce me," I told him.

He snorted. "That's only possible if she makes it all the way over here with Isla. She looks ready to bolt."

The goddess did. Her eyes were comically wide as she twisted this way and that, taking everything in. As well as having rosy cheeks, she thickly swallowed a few times when she spotted a brother with a club girl, kissing and groping each other.

We had several women around the place. I'd even admit some of the club girls were good-looking, but none of them had my attention like my little mouse did.

And fuck if I didn't give a shit that I was already thinking of her as mine.

Country snorted. "You got a bit of drool, brother."

I scratched my cheek with my middle finger. It was immature, but hell, we'd known each other since back in high school. Though Country and Death were a little older than me.

When the women got close, I straightened. Isla made her way over with a flirty smile for Country while she dragged her gaping friend behind her. The girl hadn't even noticed me or Country as yet. She was too busy gawking from side to side.

I needed her eyes on me.

Would she like the way I looked?

At least she didn't look disgusted by the brothers. A lot of us were covered in tattoos, and I was one of them.

"Yo, State" was yelled from somewhere off to the side. I knew who it was, but I wasn't giving him my attention.

I didn't look away from my mouse, so I caught her head swing our way and pause on me. I witnessed her blue eyes widening even more and how her chest rose as she sucked in a sharp breath.

Shit.

Was that good or bad? Good, I hoped.

"State," Tech yelled again, and I had to force myself to look away, which was probably for the best as I didn't want to scare her.

"What?" I barked back.

Tech nodded toward the hall.

Fuck.

It meant he had shit he needed to tell me.

"Hey, honey," I heard Isla purr at Country.

"Woman," he replied, but I could tell he was distracted.

Glancing back at the prez, I told him, "Let you know if you're needed."

He grunted. "Make sure you do."

"You know I will." I moved off toward the hall, unable to look at her again, not when there was business to deal with. There was also a chance I wouldn't want to leave once I started talking to her.

Hell, I could be overthinking and letting my cock rule me when it came to my attraction to her. But her image was embedded in my mind and left me wanting to see what was behind the looks.

Reaching Tech's room, I stepped through the door and closed it after me.

"Sorry to pull you away from your droolin', brother." His lips twitched.

"Christ, did everyone notice?"

"Who cares if they did? Just means they saw your interest and won't step on your toes."

Hell, that was a good thing.

Until I knew what she could be for me, after I had the chance to speak to her.

Jesus, I felt jittery on the inside, wanting to get back out there, see her, talk to her.

Had she put a damn spell on me?

Tech walked from his desk over to the one with the bigger monitor. He sat and wheeled the chair in close before he clicked the mouse. "Do you know this guy?"

I eyed the screen. "Pretty sure he's a client of one of the girls at Polished." All the men who visited our brothel were well vetted to be safe for the employees. "From what I can remember, he's a cop."

Tech cursed under his breath. "He's been spotted outside the clubhouse a couple of times. Nothin' that stood out because he was never there that long. But after gettin' his car plates, I put in a search from the cameras around town."

"And? Polished is legal. We have all the documents. He can't do shit about shuttin' us down," I said when he didn't answer right away.

"I don't think it's got to do with the business." Tech clicked the computer keys a few times.

When a new image popped up, I clenched my jaw and bit out, "What the fuck?"

Tech nodded. "He's made an appearance outside your home three times this week. Somethin's happened that's given him a hard-on for you. Have any idea why?"

Straightening, I crossed my arms over my chest and let my mind wander. For the life of me, I couldn't think of a situation where it'd call for a cop, who was also a client at Polished, to tail me.

"It'd have to be connected to Polished somehow. It's the only place we have in common. I've never dealt with the guy personally. You know we only step in if the clients are treatin' the women wrong. Bring up the clients list and see who he's matched with."

"Got it." Tech's fingers flew over the keyboard, and a moment later, we had an answer. "His name's Ray Bond. He joined six months ago, been with a couple of different girls, but lately he's a recurrin' customer for Ana. Real name is Lisa McRae."

"She's usually workin' on my shifts when I manage, but she's never complained about a client. Not one." I ran a hand over the back of my neck. This shit wasn't making sense, but we had to figure it out. I didn't like a cop being my personal stalker. "It's still early. Call Lisa. Set up a meetin' for me tomorrow, midafternoon at Polished. We'll see if she knows anythin'."

"Will do. I'll keep an eye on him."

"Thanks, brother."

Tech nodded toward the door. "Go get a drink. Flirt with that woman, and don't stress about this fucker. We'll get to the bottom of it."

I tipped my chin up at him. "On it. Call me for anythin'."

He saluted me before I made my way back out into the common room. My gut clenched at the thought of someone watching me. At least I knew this cop couldn't come after the club. We kept a clean ship and made sure nothing came back to us, no matter what we dealt in.

Country saw me first. He had Isla under his arm, and her friend stood facing them and away from me and my approach.

For now, I'd push away the shit about the cop and enjoy myself. I hoped to get to know my little mouse.

"Everythin' good, brother?" Country asked when I stopped behind Isla's friend, who jolted and looked over her shoulder at me.

I winked down at her before looking at Country. "All good. Talk later about it."

"All right then. State, meet Courtney. Courtney, meet State."

Courtney.

I liked it.

She moved to the side of our group and peered up at me. "Hi, ah, State."

"Hey, darlin'."

"Courtney is a friend of mine, State, so be nice," Isla said with a smile.

"I'm always nice," I replied, but I didn't glance away from Courtney, giving me the chance to see the red haze brightening her cheeks. "How'd Isla convince you to come party with us, Courtney?"

Isla was a different brand of woman to Courtney. How'd they become friends? Isla was flirty and lively. She wore a short skirt and low-cut top, with boots that came up to her knees. I could already see Courtney was quieter and reserved. She was dressed in jeans and a plain black tee. She even wore sneakers. I couldn't judge too quick, though, since I was going off one glance.

Courtney shot Isla a quick glare. So there was fire in there. She looked up at me but shifted her eyes off to the side when she said, "She didn't exactly tell me where we were going."

Well, shit.

"Does that mean you wanna leave? Can understand this could be too much for some."

She jutted her chin up and placed her hands on her hips. My little mouse had claws. "I didn't say it was too much, just unexpected. I'm…. I don't judge like that. Each to their own, and all that jazz."

Grinning, I nodded toward the bar. "Can I get you a drink then?"

She blinked. "Oh, ah, sure."

"What do you like?"

"Cranberry and vodka?"

I smirked. "Are you asking or telling me?" I didn't care what she drank, if that was what she was worried about.

"Telling. Please." She glanced at her friend, but Isla was too busy whispering into Country's ear. Not that he was paying much attention to what she was saying. His gaze was on a certain club girl who was playing poker with Quake. He seriously had to sort out his head about Dusty before one of the brothers, who didn't see her as a sister, decided to take a chance at claiming her as an old lady. She was one of the few girls who didn't try to play us.

Turning to the bar, I called the order and faced Courtney again. "How do you and Isla know each other?"

"We studied at the same beauty school a while ago. Now she does hair at a different salon to where I do nails, but we catch up for coffee every now and then." She glanced to the side, noting Isla and Country were busy, and looked back to me. "Do you, ah, work?"

"Yeah, babe."

Her lips thinned, and she lifted a hand to roll it around. "Will you elaborate? Or wait—is your job something I'm not supposed to know about?"

Chuckling, I shook my head. "You can know. I'm co-owner of Polished Pussies."

"Of what?" she breathed.

"Polished Pussies. A brothel."

"A brothel?"

"Yep."

"As in, where women sell their bodies to men?"

I nodded and waited for her to either freak out or be disgusted.

She scraped her bottom lip with her top teeth as she thought about it. Disgust was yet to show on her face, and she didn't seem too freaked by the business.

"Drinks," a prospect called behind me.

"Thanks," I muttered, but I refused to take my attention away from Courtney.

She sucked in a breath, met my gaze, and asked, "Just how much of a mess would the rooms be in after a session?" Her damn cute nose screwed up as if she was imagining being the one cleaning them.

An abrupt laugh fell from my mouth, and Christ, I wanted to drag her into my arms, but instead, I grabbed her drink and handed it to her. Her fingers slid over mine when she took it, and I didn't miss the shiver passing over her body.

That was a good shiver, right?

Smirking, I winked. "It's not somethin' you need to know, little mouse."

She'd just cemented my need to get to know her more, and already I was fucking looking forward to it.

CHAPTER TWO

Courtney

*L*ittle mouse?

I was short, but I wasn't mouse-size. Though, compared to his tall and large frame, I was at a disadvantage when it came to reprimanding him for his choice of nickname. To be honest, I'd been worried he thought I was some uptight prim woman who stuck her nose up at the visuals before me.

And there was a lot to take in since there were women pawing all over the men around me. Of course the men didn't seem to mind at all. One just grabbed a handful of a woman's butt while he kissed her like she was his favorite candy.

I wouldn't mind being kissed like that.

My cheeks warmed when I imagined State being the man who kissed me that way.

I'd be bat-shit crazy if I tried to deny he was a good-looking guy. His looks—dark hair that was shaved at the side but long enough on top that I could easily grab it and pull—made it hard to look away from him. The beard and moustache were neatly trimmed around his full lips, drawing my attention to his sinful mouth.

Heck, even his pierced nose was sexy, and I loved studying his tattoos. They decorated almost every inch of available skin that I could see from the neck down. I had to work hard to not look like a creep by just full-on staring at him. To top it all off, his deep voice made me flustered, but I was sure I was acting as cool as a cucumber.

I hoped I was, anyway. That was if he wasn't still thinking I couldn't be a part of his world.

Not that it mattered.

He was out of my league. But that didn't mean I couldn't enjoy his company while my so-called friend tried to get into her boyfriend's pants.

At least I'd made State laugh. A sound I'd enjoyed as well as the touch of lightness that came into his dark eyes.

I took a sip of my drink and choked.

State grabbed the glass in one hand and put the other on my back, patting me.

"Sorry," I wheezed.

"Prospect," he snapped.

I waved a hand around frantically. "It's fine," I

rasped. "I'm just not used to drinking." *Not used to drinking.* I mentally rolled my eyes at myself. Like I didn't do it every day. "Alcohol," I added quickly.

"It's not okay," State bit out. "Make another fuckin' drink."

"Yes, State," the younger guy said with a big gulp.

"You all right, Court?" Isla asked.

"Yeah, fine now." I was only embarrassed. I rubbed at my chest and glanced up at State, who was watching the guy pour me another drink with a glare. Reaching out, I touched his wrist, and his gaze shot down to me. "It's okay," I whispered.

His jaw clenched, but he nodded. He leaned over the counter and snapped up a bottle of water, handing it to me. The gesture was sweet.

"Thanks." I smiled and undid the bottle, taking a sip. It was then I realized he still had his hand against my back. My skin was warm under his touch. The urge to press back against it was a persistent whisper in my ear. I held strong, though. The last thing I wanted to do was embarrass myself further. There was little doubt in my mind that he was only being nice.

Only my heart didn't get the memo. It fluttered to life.

It was totally inappropriate to want that hand to travel down to my big ass. I wasn't a slim girl like a lot of the women in the room. I had curves in what I liked to think of as all the right places—hips, tits, ass, and belly. The men I'd previously dated hadn't agreed, though, being turned off by said curves.

But I loved who I was and how I looked.

All it meant was that those men weren't for me.

And I doubted the one beside me could be for me either. With that in mind, I decided I'd simply enjoy the moment, the feel of his hand on me, while I could.

"Court," Isla muttered as she got close, swaying slightly. She had acted tipsy when I'd picked her up for the night, but now she seemed a little more gone, and she hadn't even had a drink yet. "You mind if I disappear for a moment?" She nodded back to her man.

She was going to leave me alone.

She'd told me she wouldn't.

She'd promised me.

My throat closed over as a wave of nerves gripped me.

"Come on, you'll be fine." She nodded toward State, who was watching the young guy bring my new drink over.

What she didn't seem to care about was that I'd only just met the man. State seemed nice, but... this place was new to me, these people were as well, and sometimes my anxiety got the best of me in unfamiliar situations.

It was a bad idea to come with her. I shouldn't have. Lately, she'd been so different, but she'd talked me into going out with her, complaining that we hadn't done it in a long time and she missed me. The guilt had gotten the better of me, which was how I ended up here.

"Isla, we'll hang out here for a while," Country said

as he hooked the back of her skirt and dragged her close to him.

"But—"

"You can't leave your girl in a place she's not used to," State put in, handing me my new glass. I sent the prospect a smile, and he nodded at me.

Isla's laugh sounded fake, and so did her follow-up smile. She was annoyed, but I wasn't about to give in. She'd wanted me to come with her because, apparently, she hated the distance that'd grown between us. But since all she wanted to do was ditch me, I was no longer buying it.

Honestly, it reminded me why I'd stopped spending time with her. She was headed in a different direction than I was. She still loved to party every weekend and spend all her money, while I wanted more in life than dealing with a hangover after a weekend of getting drunk. Why had she wanted me to come here in the first place? To show off that she hung out at a biker club?

Maybe I'd be better without her company for the night. I could have a couple of drinks and talk to whoever took pity on me. My heart skipped a few beats at the thought. But I also didn't want to come across like I was worried about being alone in a clubhouse.

My hand shook a little when I lifted the glass and took a sip of courage. "Actually, Isla, you go do what you have to do. I'll be fine."

The change in her was instant. "Really? Are you sure you don't mind?" She bounced on her feet.

I didn't care *now* as I'd never let her put me in this position ever again. Though, from the way Country's upper lip raised as he looked at Isla, I had a feeling he was seeing her in a new light.

I nodded. "Go for it."

She turned to Country but stumbled and fell into him. He quickly grabbed her arms, steadied her, and tipped her head up with fingers under her chin. My brows dipped in confusion as he studied her face.

"You high?"

My back shot straight, my eyes widening.

Was she?

Isla laughed like he'd said the funniest thing, playfully slapping his chest. "What? No, I'm just happy." She went onto her tippytoes to kiss him, but he pulled his head back.

"Don't fuckin' lie to me, Isla. Are. You. High?" His tone had me taking a small step back.

"Country," she whined. "You're ruining my buzz."

"Coke? Heroin? Ice? What did you take?"

She snorted, shaking her head. "I'm going to dance."

She must have taken it just before I got to her house. The thought made me feel ill.

Country grabbed her upper arm, and he focused on State. "I'm takin' her to lie down."

Isla cheered. "Bedroom fun." She curled herself around Country as he led her off.

I highly doubted she was going to get the fun she thought she was. Would it be better if I took her home instead? I was supposed to be her friend and save her from a ranting Country in the morning, right? I couldn't help but think she deserved a good talking to, and I doubted I'd be the one to get through to her.

When State rested a hand on the back of my shoulder, I jolted. "She'll be fine. Country will make sure she sleeps it off. He won't do shit to her. We aren't—"

"I wasn't thinking that," I quickly said. "I just wasn't sure if I was supposed to be the supporting friend and save her from an argument in the morning with her guy or leave her and let her suffer."

His lips twitched. "I'm guessin' you're goin' with the last one?"

Sighing, I nodded. "Does that make me a bad friend?"

"Nah, darlin'."

"Are you sure? I mean, we kind of drifted apart recently, and when she asked me to come out with her, I caved because I knew it was my fault we'd been distant…. Why am I telling you this?" I took a heavy mouthful of my drink and swallowed. "Sorry."

"She was ready to leave your ass in a place you've never been, and around a bunch of bikers, just to get it on with her man. If I were you, I wouldn't feel bad over leavin' Country to deal with her shit in the mornin'."

Well, she definitely was going to do that.

"I suppose." I nodded.

"Who drove here?"

"I did, thankfully."

"Smart. But now it's up to you if you want to leave,

or you can hang and shoot the shit with me while you finish your drink. No pressure."

Even if he hadn't said no pressure, I'd already known there wouldn't be.

Drawing in a breath, I said, "I'd like to finish my drink."

The smile he shot my way brought the fluttering to life in my belly.

"Wanna grab a seat with me?" He nodded toward a spare table. When I bobbed my head, he led us over there with his hand warming my lower back again.

My pulse raced, and I shivered. This man was too attractive for his own good.

But I wouldn't believe there could be anything between us. It would be easy to get caught up in the fantasy of the hot biker. Still, I wanted to enjoy his company, even if it was only for the night.

When we sat, I took another sip of my drink. Since I was driving, one would do, but I wanted to make it last.

"Do you have any family?" I asked. "I mean, besides the group here."

He grinned. "They're my brothers here. But other than them, I don't have anyone. My mom and dad passed away a few years ago. Only a couple of months apart. When Dad lost Mom to cancer, I knew he wouldn't be far behind. She was his world."

That kind of love was what I wanted in my life. I smiled softly. "Sorry to hear you lost them."

He shrugged. "Shit happens."

"That it does. My parents are that in love too. I could see the same thing happening with them."

"You're close with them?"

"Yes." I nodded. "I see them every Sunday for family dinner. My brothers try and make it, if they're not busy."

"How many are there?"

"Three. Carter, Calvin, and Casper."

His dark brows shot up. "Your parents must really like the letter C."

A laugh fell from my lips. "I guess they do."

He took a pull of his beer, and I watched his throat work. It was unfair how good-looking this man was. He made my body come alive. I wanted to offer myself up as a sacrifice, but I couldn't be his. There wasn't a chance that would be happening.

Not only were we worlds apart, but he was probably only looking for a one-night stand. I couldn't give in to even that. If I did, I'd become addicted.

Instead, I'd admire him for the night while we chatted. He was good company.

One night of talking. I could allow myself that.

And hope it didn't leave me wanting more.

CHAPTER THREE

State

As I twisted the pen in my fingers, I leaned back in my office chair and waited on Lisa. But my mind wasn't on the stalker cop. It was on the woman who'd ditched me the previous night when I'd gone to the bathroom.

I'd thought we'd been connecting.

I'd thought there could be something there that could grow.

So why did she walk out?

We'd been getting to know each other.

We'd been laughing.

All my attention had been on her and hers on me.

Even when brothers tried to get in our damn

bubble, she smiled politely, said what she had to, but her gaze kept coming back to me.

What changed?

What had she been thinking to run out of there?

The door opened, and Country stepped in. "Tech told me what's happenin'. I'm here to see what Lisa's got to say. She's got to be the connection." He took a seat on the couch on the far wall. We shared this office with Wreck, another brother, while the fourth co-owner, Saint, had his own office on the ground floor. One of us was always on hand to deal with any complaints or troubles, but it didn't surprise me that Country wanted to be involved in this. He was a good prez.

"That was my thought too. How'd it go this morning with Isla?"

He shot me a glare. "Shit."

I whistled long and low.

"Her friend didn't seem to be high."

"From what I gathered, they hadn't hung out for a while. Drifted. But Court felt bad when Isla begged her to go out, so she did."

He grunted and ran a hand over his face. "Isla's changed. Somethin's goin' on with her, and I'm gonna get to the bottom of it."

"Let me know if you need help."

He waved me off. "Isla's girl stay long while I dealt with her?" He started chuckling. "That smile says a lot."

I shrugged. "We talked. Thought it was cool until she left while I was takin' a piss."

Another round of laughter. "Brother, she ghosted you?"

"Yeah, and I don't get it."

"Huh."

"Huh what?"

He eased back further and placed his arm across the back of the couch while resting his ankle on his other knee. "You into her?"

I pushed my hair back and nodded. "Hard not to be. She's sweet, funny, smart, and got a fuckin' bangin' body."

"Wasn't around her long, but I got the idea she liked the look of you. How long she stay for?"

"About two hours."

"Fuck, brother, that's a good amount of time to get to know each other. Hell, maybe what she was feelin' was scarin' her, so she took off. Did you get her number?"

"Didn't get the chance to."

"What you gonna do?"

"Chase."

He smirked. "Never thought I'd see the day when State's ready to chase."

I shot him the middle finger. "She's worth it."

His brows shot up. "You're sayin' that after one night? Shit, I've been with Isla for nearly a month, and I'm not even sure she's worth it. 'Specially now."

"Then she ain't."

"That simple?"

"That simple. You know who is special—"

"Shut the fuck up."

"Just sayin'—"

"Not another word," he clipped with a glower.

Christ, when was he going to get his head out of his ass about Dusty?

Luckily for him, or probably myself, because if I'd said more my life would be on the line, there was a knock on the door.

"In," I called.

The door opened, and Lisa poked her head in. "You wanted to see me?"

"Yeah, babe. Come on in."

She did and shut the door. When she walked over to the seat in front of my desk, she kept glancing from me to Country and back again. "Am I in trouble?"

"Not at all. Just gotta ask you some questions about a client."

Her shoulders slumped, tension draining out. Hell, Country and I weren't that intimidating, were we?

Lisa nodded. "Okay."

"Ray Bond."

Her long sigh said a lot.

"You had problems with him?"

"Well, no, not really. He's a little obsessed. Tells me he loves me, wants me to quit here and marry him. Is he causing trouble with the business? I swear I haven't encouraged him. I even told him I have a boyfriend who would kill him if he found out Ray was asking me to marry him."

"Did you give Ray the name of your boyfriend?" Country asked.

She nodded and went a little pale.

"Lisa?" I pressed.

"I only said I was with you because you're my boss. Well, the one who deals with me on my shift, and I panicked when no other name came to me. I'm sorry." She dropped her gaze to her lap.

"You told him I'm your man?" I asked, to be clear.

"Yes. Look, I can set him straight, but if I do and he finds out I don't have a boyfriend, he'll start pestering me about being with him. I don't want him like that. Sometimes he pays me extra. I know you guys don't mind if that happens with clients. But the bonus he gives me is the only reason I haven't said anything or got you involved."

Country and I shared a look. At least it explained why he was stalking me. He thought I was competition. But how far would he go to try and get rid of me?

"We're gonna have to keep an eye on him, Lisa. He's been seen outside the compound and my own home."

She gasped, hand to her chest. "You're kidding me."

"I don't kid about shit like that."

Country drew her attention to him. "Lisa. Next time you have a session with him, let him know you and your fake boyfriend are having issues. That you might break it off with him soon. See how that goes."

"And if it doesn't help and he still stalks State?"

"Tell him you and State aren't anythin', and that you

need time on your own because you're totally heartbroken. During that time, we'll get rid of him as a client. Doesn't matter he's a cop. He ain't got different rules to anyone else here. We can end anyone's access to Polished without an excuse. He signed the forms before joinin', so if he tried anythin', we've got that at our backs."

"Okay. I'm really sorry about this."

"Honey," I started, "it ain't your fault a man's obsessin' over you. But next time somethin' like this happens, and a client gets too clingy, you need to tell us."

"I will. I promise. I thought he'd get bored with me when he knows I'm taken and won't quit."

"Obviously not the case, but let's see how this shit goes," Country said.

"Got it. I'll start by telling him we're fighting first to see if he'll stop showing up, right?"

"Yeah, babe, and in case there are any problems, make sure to have your pin on at all times. Record anythin' you think that we'll need to know, and use the goddamn alarm on it if things get out of hand."

"Promise. Can I go now?"

I waved her off, and she quickly left, closing the door behind her. "Shit, maybe we need to have a business meetin' with the girls again to reinstate the rules and to make sure they always have their pins with them." They were there for emergencies and, if pressed, it sent a signal to Death's security office, calling in for backup.

Country nodded. "Could be a good idea. Get Wreck onto settin' somethin' up."

"Saint's more approachable. I'll have him do it."

Country chuckled. "Good thinkin'. Hope this works, brother."

"So do I, because I don't want to be stuck with a cop up my ass."

Country's gaze hardened. "Not gonna happen."

I understood what he wasn't saying. We'd deal with the situation one way or another. "Yeah, brother. But let's fuckin' pray it's the smoother way."

Country snorted. "Sure would be easier for us."

I smirked. "But we don't mind a challenge either."

"Damn right." He stood and started for the door. "Good luck with findin' your woman, brother."

"Actually," I called, and Country turned back at the door. "Can you ask Isla where Courtney works?"

"Ain't she a nail person?"

"Yeah."

His laughter irritated me. "You gonna book an appointment to get your nails done?"

"No, I'll get Eve to book for me." Eve was a brother's sister who was close with the club.

He guffawed. "And you'd actually sit there for her to do your nails, wouldn't you?"

I glared. "If it came to it, yes."

"Shit, brother, you truly are gone. I'll text you when I find out."

"Thanks, and good luck with Isla."

"Yeah, I reckon I'll need it." He shot me a two-finger wave before he left.

Adrenaline pumped into my veins over the thought of seeing my little mouse again. If Country was right that she was scared about the connection we'd made, I'd settle those nerves down one way or another. No way was I missing out on a chance on seeing where we could go.

In a way, I hoped she was feeling too much from spending time with me. If so, it meant I'd gotten under her skin like she had mine.

Christ, thinking of her had my cock fattening under my jeans.

I wanted to see her smile, hear her laugh, and tuck her hair behind her ear while I leaned in for my first taste of her mouth.

I'd kept myself under control that night, not taking her like I wanted to.

But when I saw her again, I wasn't sure how restrained I could be.

She was something special.

My kind of special.

And if I had to get my damn nails done around a bunch of women while I made her understand that, I'd fucking do it.

CHAPTER FOUR

Courtney

It had been a week, and the image of State, along with his perfect rough voice, kept popping into my mind just to taunt me.

When I was cooking. *Hey, let's think about State.*

When I was watching TV. *State was better than that guy.*

When I was in bed. *Let's masturbate about State.*

Even when I was on the toilet. *State and I could be pooping at the same time right now.*

That thought was the reason I took up humming while in the bathroom.

I'd left the compound that night with a smile on my face but with my insides twisted up because I had really enjoyed State's company. We'd even talked for a couple of hours and he'd been easy to chat to—our subjects far-reaching. We'd laughed a lot over silly stories or our families. I told him a few more because I'd loved his chuckle.

And then I'd ghosted him like an idiot.

I'd wanted to ask for his number but chickened out, reminding myself that he'd never be interested in a woman like me. Heck, I'd seen the sort of women who were at the bar, and compared to them, I was a plain-Jane nun.

Sighing, I finished off my lunch and placed the container in my locker. I had a full afternoon of appointments and really had to keep my mind on the job. If I didn't, I'd end up painting State's name onto a client's nails or something equally as mortifying.

I closed the door and rested my forehead against it.

Regret filled me once more for leaving when State had gone to the bathroom. I'd been worried he'd offer to exchange numbers to be polite, and had known I wouldn't be able to refuse. But there was still the concern he'd only want one night between the sheets with me and I'd have a hankering for more. If he denied me more, it could crush me in the end.

Groaning, I banged my head against my locker.

I'd ghosted him.

Ghosted the most handsome, charming man I had ever met.

I really was an idiot.

The biggest loser in the world.

My phone chimed in my apron. I quickly pulled it out and checked the caller ID before I answered. "Mom. What's up?"

"I'm kicking him out of the house."

Smiling, I rolled my eyes. "Are we talking about Dad?"

"Yes, Courtney. Do you know what he just said to me?" Dad's laughter filtered in from the background. "It's not funny, Patty."

"It is. It really is," Dad commented.

"What did he say?"

"When I told him I saw our neighbor kiss his wife goodbye when he goes to work, I asked him why he doesn't do that. His reply," she bit out, "was how could he? He doesn't know her."

I groaned. "Mom, I've seen that joke online, and besides, Dad's retired." The door to the lunchroom opened, and Danielle stuck her head in.

"Ah, Courtney, your appointment is here."

"I'll be right there," I told her and saw her look over her shoulder and back to me before she nodded and stepped back out. "Mom, I have to go. My client's here early."

"Okay, I'll see you tomorrow, and if your father jokes like that again, don't expect him at the dinner table. He'll be buried in the backyard."

Laughing, I shook my head. "See you soon." I slipped my phone back into my pocket and straightened my clothes on the way through the double doors.

When I looked up with a smile, I froze.

State stood near my table.

State.

A big biker guy was in a salon.

The man I'd ghosted like a weirdo now stood not far away.

He was also surrounded by other clients and some work colleagues.

"Your hair is amazing. I'd love to get my hands on it," Rina, the owner of the salon, said, placing a hand on his forearm and smiling coyly up at him.

That was what got me moving.

I stomped over and gently pushed my way through the crowd to stand opposite my table. "State, hi."

He hadn't heard my approach because of all the damn hussies trying to talk over one another for his attention, but over all the noise, he'd heard me. When his gaze shot to mine, I gripped the back of my chair because his wide grin had me swooning. "Darlin', how you doin'?"

All the women glared at me, and I waved my hand toward them. "I'm sure you all have to get back to what you were doing."

They mumbled and muttered but at least went away. When I lifted my eyes to State again, I watched him pull out the chair opposite my table and sit down.

My mouth dropped open, but I quickly closed it. "Ah, what are you doing?"

"I'm your client."

"You?"

"Yep."

"You want your nails done?"

He shrugged. "Sure."

Why was he here?

Why, after I'd gone and left while he was in the bathroom?

Already my heart, my pulse, and my belly were acting up, as if all of them wanted to reach out to this man and kidnap him.

At least my head was still screwed on.

Well, I thought it was, but I couldn't get over the fact he'd come to find me at my workplace. Not after what I'd done.

This was dangerous.

If he wasn't careful, I *would* kidnap him and keep him forever.

Clearing my throat, I sat and stared down at his tattooed hands resting on the table. My face heated as I took one of his big palms and started filing his nails. I opened my mouth, closed it, and then managed to blurt, "I'm sorry for leaving like I did."

His hand twisted in mine, and he gripped my tiny hand in his large one. The pitter-patter in my chest intensified. His thumb brushed back and forth over my wrist, and I couldn't look away from it.

His tone was rough, low, and mouthwatering when he asked, "Why did you leave?"

Because I was feeling too much, which scared me.

Because I didn't want you to take pity and offer me your number.

Most of all, because you're way out of my league.

"I, um, felt it would be better." God, that sounded lamer aloud than in my head.

"Why?"

"Well, you see, you got stuck with me that night, and I didn't want you to feel you had to, ah, offer any more than what it was."

His jaw clenched. "What was it?"

I glanced around and noted people were trying to listen in. I leaned over the table more and whispered, "A night of good company and conversation."

A tick started at his temple. He shifted closer, his gaze running over my face before he locked onto my eyes. "Do you have a problem with me being in a club?"

"No," I said instantly, my hand tightening around his. "Never."

"I didn't get stuck with you, little mouse. I wanted to get to know you. I wanted to spend time with you. And fuck, I wanted to get your number to text and talk to you whenever we could, because I'd enjoyed the hell outta our time together."

I stilled and blinked up at him.

He *had* wanted my number. He'd also *liked* spending that time with *me*.

"Are you sure?" I asked before I could stop myself. I grimaced, knowing I sounded completely insecure, but my past hurt made me wary.

State cocked a brow and smirked. "Woman, where am I?"

I looked around and back to him. "In a salon."

"Yeah, darlin'. In a salon. I've never stepped foot in one since I was a kid. What does that tell you?"

I bit my bottom lip and hummed.

He chuckled. "I'll let you know, Courtney. It means I'm here for you because you didn't give me your number, and I wanna take you out sometime."

Wide-eyed, I parted my lips. "Me?"

"Yeah, little mouse. You." His brows dipped. "Why you findin' that hard to believe?"

Snorting, I waved my free hand his way. "Because you're you and I'm me."

Quit it, Courtney. You sound like you want compliments.

"We're gonna get to the bottom of that another day." He shifted closer over the table. "But let me be clear on this: as soon as I saw you walk into the compound, I knew I wanted to get to know you because, darlin', you took my whole attention like no one else has."

"Yes," I blurted, cheeks warming.

"Yes what, Courtney?"

There wasn't a chance in hell I was going to let this man walk out of there without agreeing to a date. He'd come to find me. He was obviously even willing to get his nails done. Most of all, he'd wanted to know me when he first saw me.

And damn if that wasn't a game-changer.

Swallowing, I pressed my finger against my lips and glanced around quickly. Both clients and staff were watching. How could they not when it was State? "I'd like to go on a date with you."

He showered me with another bright smile that got my blood pumping harder.

"Good to hear, little mouse. I got somethin' on tonight, which will probably take me until tomorrow, but are you busy for lunch Monday?"

"This Monday?" That was only two sleeps away.

"Yeah."

"No. I mean, I don't work Mondays, so I'm free."

"Good. You like steak?"

"Steak is nice."

"I know a place. You gonna give me your number this time?"

Heat hit my cheeks. "Yes," I whispered. "Do you have your phone on hand?"

He let go of my palm to pull his cell out of his jeans. "Hit me."

I rattled off my number and then bit my bottom lip to stop my crazed smile from scaring him. I couldn't believe he was here, at my work, to get my number and ask me out.

"Thanks, little mouse."

I heard a snort somewhere. "Little, sure. She's wider than a house." As soon as the voice penetrated, I knew who it was. Margot. She was Rina's recurring client who loved to gossip and talk shit about people. A lot.

Her comment didn't worry me; she'd been giving me "helpful" hints about new trending diets for a while. What did worry me was the way State slowly turned his hard gaze on her.

"You got somethin' to say?" he clipped.

"State—" When he took my hand, I shut up.

Margot smiled, not clueing in on his pissed-off vibe. "You could do better, handsome."

I swore everyone in the room tensed and grew silent.

"State, it's fine." I squeezed his hand.

He shook his head. "It ain't fine when a haggy old lady talks shit about someone I like." He stood with his fists pressed to the table. "How about you mind your own fuckin' business, and you might get some dick yourself because it's obvious you ain't been since you're so uptight thinkin' you have the right to talk about Courtney that way."

Margot gasped. "How dare you."

"I dare, lady." State looked at me, leaned down, and pressed his lips against mine in a firm kiss. "See you Monday."

"Okay," I breathed.

He bopped me on the nose, smiled, and walked out of the salon.

"Court," Rina called as she pulled off Margot's apron. "I have to say you are one lucky bitch. Margot, since you've already paid and your hair is done, you can go, and I think it's best you see another stylist from now on."

"You can't—"

"I can and I will to protect the people who work here."

With a huff, Margot stood and walked out of the salon with her nose in the air.

"Rina, are you sure that's a good idea?"

"Honey, I should have done that a long time ago. Now, since you have time, come on back and tell me what you're going to wear on your date."

Oh God, I had a date.

A date with State.

Ha, that rhymes.

Jesus, I hoped I wasn't a bundle of nerves by the time Monday came around.

CHAPTER FIVE

Courtney

As soon as I entered the kitchen for Sunday family dinner, Mom pounced on me. "You're glowing. Patty, don't you think she's glowing?"

"Sure. Hi, princess."

"Hi, Dad."

Mom gasped. "Are you pregnant?"

Casper snorted. "She has to have sex to be pregnant." My hand, all on its own, whipped out and smacked him in the back of the head. "Shit. I'm kidding, sis."

"Language," Mom snapped. She called us out on our cussing all the time, but it always slipped out. I

37

wondered how she'd go with State since he swore like a trooper. The thought of them meeting had me smiling.

"Maybe she is getting a bit. See that smile," Carter put in.

"Can we not discuss your sister getting anything," Dad barked and shuddered.

"Everyone has sex, Patty," Mom told him like he didn't already know.

Rolling my eyes, I ignored them all and hugged Mom, then Casper, since he was the closest, followed by Calvin, Dad, and Carter. To whom I said, "Good to see you here, my big professional sports brother."

Carter scratched his chin with his middle finger, even though he was the oldest and supposed to be the most mature. "As I ask you every damn time, how long are you going to call me that?"

"A few more years yet."

"It's bad enough you show up to games with that on a sign. The guys on the team give me shit—"

"Language."

"—about it all the time."

Grinning a little evilly, I scooped food onto my plate. "It's what sisters are for."

He leaned in. "And brothers are for this." He cleared his throat. "You know what, Mom. I think you're right. Court could be glowing from being pregnant."

Mom's fork dropped from her hand. "Are you?" she near screeched. That was just mean of Carter. He knew, like all of us, she was desperately waiting to have grandbabies.

"No, Mom, I'm not. I do have a date tomorrow, though."

"Who is he?" Carter demanded.

"What's his name?" Calvin asked, taking out his phone.

"Does he have a job at least?" Dad queried.

"Warn him you snore," Casper put in.

"I do not," I yelled at him.

His brow rose. "I was in the room next to you for many years. You do."

"Shut up." I glared.

"Who is this man, and where did you meet him?" Mom asked.

"I'll tell you more about him later, Mom. Not when the evil lot are listening in. They'll try and find him and warn him away, but I like this one."

Carter scoffed. "You said that about Josh, and he was sleeping with his stepmom."

Mom gasped. "Was he?"

"She also said that about Keith, and he was collecting porcelain dolls and hoped Courtney would dress like one if she lost some weight." My brothers, and even my dad, grumbled about some of my dating attempts that were epic fails.

In fairness, I hadn't seen Keith's collection until he took me to his place after we'd been dating a month. He had been nice and never pressured me into anything. Not until he confessed I was too big and needed to resemble one of "his girls." I'd never run out of a house so fast. It was lucky Calvin had been in the area and picked me up. After he'd told Keith to never call me again, or if he did, they'd have issues, a pale Keith had nodded and stepped into his house, engaging all his locks.

"Can we not talk about them?" I pleaded.

Mom patted my hand. "Tell me later."

"Not fair," Casper complained. "At least give us a name."

I took a mouthful of peas and corn and mumbled around it.

"Boys, leave your sister alone. Besides, I'll tell you later when I have the information off your mom."

"Dad!" I yelled. "Mom?"

"Sweetie, I won't tell him anything." I watched her mouth to Dad, "I'll tell you later."

Pointing my fork at her and then Dad, I reprimanded, "You know I can see you."

Mom just smiled and patted my arm. "I have only one question. Does he want children?"

"First date, Mom. This will be our *first* date."

"All right, fine. Now, Carter?"

"I'm not seeing anyone, Mom."

"Calvin, have you and Jena talked about—"

"She dumped me because she was more in love with her job than with me." Calvin hunched over his plate and shoveled food into his mouth.

"Oh" was Mom's wise reply.

"Do you need me to beat her up?" I offered.

"Courtney," Mom exclaimed.

Calvin gave me a soft smile. "Nah, I just don't want to talk about it."

"I mean, she's a trollop for leaving my son, but what do you mean, more in love with her job?"

We loved our mom, but sometimes she didn't know when to leave things alone, and I could really tell Calvin didn't want to talk about it. He'd go to Dad later. Alone. So I took one for the team.

"His name's State. Well, that's his club name. I don't know his real name yet. I do know I like him, because when I met him at the compound, and after Isla left me to fend for myself, he spent the time talking to me. Then I ghosted him, letting myself sink into my doubts. However, he made an appointment at the salon to get his nails done just so he could talk to me and ask me out. He told me that when I walked into the compound, he knew that he wanted to get to know me because I took his whole attention like no one else has before." I took a deep breath and then went on. "He also shut Margot down"— they all knew about her—"when she told him he could do better. He called her haggy and told her if she ever said anything about me again, they were going to have problems." My hand shook when I took a sip of water.

Mom sniffed.

"Mom," I whispered, amused.

She waved a hand around. "Hormones."

I looked at Dad, worried about his opinion since I'd outed State as being in a motorcycle club. I didn't care, and I hoped he wouldn't.

He smiled warmly. "Good luck on your date, princess."

Warmth spread through me. My family was amazing.

"Don't mess this up, sis. I want an invite to the compound. I heard women fall at their feet." Everyone stared at Casper. He shrugged. "What? It's just what I heard."

"There is no way I would take you there," I told him.

"What about me?" Carter asked.

"I wouldn't mind going either," Calvin added.

I threw up a hand. "I haven't even gone on a date with him yet."

Mom shook her head. "Ignore them. I hope things go well, and we look forward to meeting him."

Yeah, that wouldn't be for a long time. I didn't want to scare him off.

LATER, when I was sitting on my couch in my one-bedroom apartment, my phone chimed, and my heart skipped a beat. I nearly fell off the couch with how quickly I moved to grab it off the coffee table in front of me.

State: How was your day, little mouse?

Thank God no one was around to see how my face nearly cracked with how big I was smiling.

Me: Good. Just got back from dinner with the family. What about yours?

State: Boring. How'd dinner go?

I bit my bottom lip.

Me: Well, my brothers now want an invite to the compound.

There was a pause, and worry seeped in. Did I say something wrong? Did I spell it wrong? I quickly read over my words. Then jumped when it chimed. I scrolled to his message.

State: You told them about me?

Sitting straighter, I pressed my fingers to my lips. Was I not supposed to?

Me: I did. I hope you don't mind.

State: Nah, little mouse. Was it just your brothers around?

Me: No, my parents were there.

State: Good.

Was it?

State: Like you sharin' about me, darlin'. Your brothers can come to the next party.

Me: Don't say that!!!! You haven't met them. They can be very embarrassing. For me.

State: I'll make sure they won't be. Got to go, baby. Lookin' forward to seein' you tomorrow. You know where the place is?

Me: I do. I'll be there at 12.

State: Night, little mouse.

Me: Night. I added a smiley face and then regretted it. *Do bikers like smiley faces?* Was it too much?

Groaning, I slumped back on the couch, squishing my chin to my neck. Yeah, this would be a real pretty look for State to see me in with all my double-chin glory.

But… he liked me, or else he wouldn't have come to find me.

He didn't mind I was short.

He didn't mind I was plus-size, or a nail technician, or that I have three brothers, or that I usually said what I was thinking.

He liked me.

When my phone rang, scaring the shit out of me, I let out a yell. Picking it up, I looked at the caller ID.

Isla.

Shit.

I wasn't ready to deal with her even after a week, especially as she hadn't reached out to explain why she had wanted to abandon me and was apparently high that night. Why would she get high before going out with me in the first place when she knew I wasn't a fan of people on hard drugs? Marijuana was all right. Not that I'd tell my parents I thought that, or that I'd even had some on a few of my wilder nights out. Though, it turned out my "wild night" was me getting the giggles for absolutely no reason and then getting so tired I'd just wanted to sleep.

Did I ignore her call or deal with her?

Sighing, I scrubbed a hand over my face and then pressed the green button. "Hi, Isla."

"Court, I didn't think you would answer. I'm so sorry for how I acted at the compound. Country ripped me a new asshole about it. I should never have even suggested leaving you alone there. I promise I'll never do it again."

"What were you on?" I asked quietly.

She laughed. "That doesn't matter. I know not to take it when I'm around you, Miss Goody Two-shoes."

That stung. We used to be thick as thieves, but she didn't need to be condescending just because I'd gone down a different path than her.

"Isla, why are you even—"

"I don't want a lecture from you. I told Country I'd apologize, and I did. God, Court, I heard you had a good night with State anyway. You should be thanking *me* for introducing you. Not that I thought you'd have a chance with— Fuck, Court, I didn't mean that. Look, I'm just going through a rough patch and can be a bitch without thinking. You'll forgive me, right?"

Would I?

No. Not anymore.

But she didn't need to know that. "Sure, Isla. Look, I have to go. We'll talk soon."

"We won't, will we? One mistake and you're ready to drop our friendship."

Closing my eyes, I dropped my head back. An ache started at my temples. I hated confrontation or hurting anyone's feelings, but maybe it was time I stuck to honesty.

"We've been drifting apart for a while, Isla. I want to settle down soon and start a family. You want to stay partying. It's okay. This happens when we're into different things."

"I suppose you're right. You were always a bore." With that, she hung up.

I wouldn't let her words get to me, because she was right about one thing. I wouldn't have met State if it wasn't for her, and I was grateful for that.

CHAPTER SIX

State

I stood out in front of the steakhouse with my hands in my jeans, leaning against the wall. Hell, I couldn't wait to see my little mouse, but I also had other shit on my mind that I needed to push back before she arrived. Lisa had carried out the plan with the cop, but I was still getting visits. Weirdest thing was, he didn't do anything, and the one time, when I went to approach him, he just drove off. Lisa was going to step up the game tomorrow night when he was at Polished and tell him we'd broken up.

It'd better do something because I didn't want this crap around Courtney.

I didn't even know how he'd react if he was out

there now watching me, waiting to see what I was standing around for. What would he do if he saw me with Courtney? It worried me enough my gut was in knots.

He'd better stay the fuck away from Courtney.

I'd have to tell her what was going on in case he didn't. It'd be stupid to keep it from her. She had to be warned.

Movement down the road caught my attention.

Fuck me.

All other thoughts evaporated when my gaze landed on Courtney. She looked stunning in her flowery summer dress that hugged her in all the right places.

How in the hell had she not been snapped up already and dating someone?

It was good she wasn't, or I'd have to kill them.

Christ, even the thought of someone else in her life like that got my blood boiling.

I started toward her and caught when she noticed me. My throat fucking thickened at the smile she graced me with.

She was happy to see me.

Jesus, we still had a lot of getting to know each other to do, but I already felt the need to put a ring on her finger as soon as possible. I didn't think attraction this deep could happen from first sight. Yet, it did. For me, at least.

"Little mouse," I said, dipping to kiss the corner of her mouth, and I felt her tiny gasp. She gripped my forearm where I'd put it around her waist and breathed out a shaky breath.

My cock jerked, and when I straightened, she blinked up at me, almost like she was out of it. "State," she murmured.

"Hey, darlin'." I grinned, and for some reason, it had her sucking in a breath. Christ, she was gorgeous. "Ready for food?"

"Food?"

Chuckling, I nodded. "Yeah, Court. Steak."

She blinked and shook her head a little. "Oh, um, yes. I'm ready for steak."

"Good." I took her hand in mine and led her into the front of the restaurant. I'd wanted to pick her up and drop her home, but I didn't want to force anything or make her feel uncomfortable, like I was looking at more than just a first date to get to know her more.

"Welcome to Laws. How can I help you?"

"Booking under State."

He took a moment to look in the book. "Ah yes." He clicked his fingers, and a young waiter guy stepped up. I glanced at Courtney to see her jaw clenched.

When I had her eyes and raised my brows, she shook her head.

"This is Mitchell. He'll be taking care of your section." He looked at Mitchell and frowned, then went ahead and straightened the guy's tie in front of us. Mitchell went red while the guy muttered about Mitchell not being able to dress himself.

I'd never been here before; I'd just heard it had good steak, but this fucker was souring my mood.

He nodded to Mitchell, who turned and started forward. I went to lead Court away with a hand to her back, but she stopped at the front desk, leaned in and said, "Just because he's young doesn't mean you can treat him like he's beneath you and belittle him in front of people. And no one should click their fingers at someone like they're an animal. That shows what type of person *you* are."

She gave him one last look before stalking off, and I couldn't help but grin like a maniac. I would have said something about his attitude, but I'd worried how Court would take it. I'd already caused a shitshow in her work, something I needed to apologize for. I didn't want to do it there.

However, I didn't have to.

My little mouse had already taken it in hand.

At the table, we took our seats. Mitchell leaned down. "Thank you," he whispered to Court.

She smiled up at him, and his eyes widened. Fuck me, the kid was about to get a crush. Court patted his hand. "He was a pompous ass, so it was my pleasure."

Just as he went to lay his hand over hers, I cleared my throat. His gaze swung to me, and I shook my head. He straightened and handed out the menus. "Can I get you started on a drink while you look over the menu?"

"Beer, anything on tap. Court?"

"Um, Diet Coke, please."

"Right away."

He disappeared, and I placed my menu down. When my little mouse noticed, she put hers on the table and met my eyes. "I'm sorry about saying something, but he was—"

"Darlin', don't apologize for that. You're right. He was an ass. I would have said somethin' myself, but I'd worried I'd done enough damage at your work. I was gonna bring it up in a text, but I thought it would be better in person. Did I fuck things up at work for you?"

Tension coiled inside me. Christ, if I had, I'd be worse than the guy at the front of the restaurant.

Her smile brightened my damn life. "No. Rina, my boss who wanted to get her hands on your hair, ended up kicking Margot out and telling her not to come back."

I sat back as shock slipped in. "You're shittin' me?"

She laughed and shook her head. "I'm not."

"That's all right then. I wasn't sure if you would've been embarrassed by me and how I acted."

"State, no. I met you at a biker compound. If you haven't figured it out already, I know you speak your mind, with a few cuss words thrown in, and I can already tell you'll protect those close to you."

Christ, she was starting to figure me out, and how I lived my life didn't seem to bother her. We were at the early stages, but already she was showing me there was a high chance she could handle my world.

"You're somethin' else, little mouse."

I smirked when she blushed and tried to wave me off.

"Darlin', if this goes where I want it to go, there are things you need to know about me, about the club."

"Okay, but, um, where do you see this going?"

"For a fuckin' long way in the future."

"Oh," she breathed and glanced at the table. I wasn't sure if she was trying to hide her smile or not, but I saw it, and my gut turned in a good way knowing she liked the idea of us being in this for the long run.

Mitchell appeared at our sides and placed our drinks down. "Are you both ready to order?"

I glanced at Court.

"I am if you are."

I smirked. "You didn't get long to even look at the menu."

She shrugged. "I know what I want." Her gaze held mine for a long moment.

"Good."

Mitchell cleared his throat. Court startled and picked up the menu. "Right, I'll have the ribeye, medium to well done, with a mushroom sauce, and vegetables for the side, please."

"Ribeye for me too, but rare to medium, with the pepper sauce. Fries and salad." I grabbed Court's menu and handed them both back to Mitchell.

"Won't be long." Mitchell smiled and walked off.

"Isla rang me last night," she blurted, and then thinned her lips into a tight smile.

"How'd that go?"

She blew out a breath and tucked some of her hair behind one ear. Already I could tell she didn't like the phone call. Annoyance threaded into my blood. Country had been right about his woman. She was changing, and if that change hurt Court, I'd have a word with Isla myself.

"She apologized, and other things were said, but in the end, I doubt we'll be seeing each other again. She's mad that I don't agree with her life choices."

"She say anythin' bad?"

"Nothing I can't handle and know is a lie. I'm…. It's just with her dating Country, and if you invite me back to the compound with her there, it might not go down well."

"There's no *if* I invite you back. It'll happen, but I'll make sure she won't be around. To be honest, Country didn't like how she acted either. She's been different for a while. Eventually, he'll see she ain't for him. But let me know if she comes at you for anythin', yeah?"

"I will."

"Thanks, darlin'." Leaning back in the chair, I grinned. "Though I can't be too cut with Isla. She did bring me you."

Her pupils dilated, her breath coming out in pants, but with a shake of her head, she cleared her throat and nodded, looking off to the side. "I thought the same thing." Her gaze flicked to mine. "I mean about you. That she brought you to me. Wait, I mean…." She sighed. "You know what I mean."

Chuckling, I tipped my chin up at her. "Yeah, little mouse. I know."

I tensed and straightened, looking over at the entrance when I heard a commotion starting.

Ray fucking Bond with another few officers stalked my way.

"You've got to be fuckin' kiddin' me." I stood up and stepped in front of my woman as she climbed to her feet.

"State?"

"Whatever they say, it's shit. Don't believe them, Courtney." I quickly handed her my phone behind my back. "Call Country, passcode 1209. This cop, Ray Bond, remember his name, thinks I'm doin' his Polished girl. I'm *not*. Just call Country."

"I will." Her tone was weak, full of fear. Anger wrapped around me. This goddamn prick was going to get what was coming to him for interrupting this date.

"It'll be all right, baby."

"Okay."

"Dominic Miller, you are under arrest for the suspicion of murdering James Sullen. Place your hands on your head."

I did but looked over my shoulder. "Call Country. I didn't do this."

A cop pulled me around and snapped my arms down to handcuff me.

"You have the right to remain silent."

Now that I was facing Court, I saw worry was more present than fear. "Courtney, I didn't do this."

She straightened, jutting her chin up. "I know."

"Anything you say may be used against you in the court of law."

I tuned them out and just looked at Courtney while she kept my gaze.

"I'll call Country. I'll get you help. Don't worry."

"I'm not, darlin'."

She smiled, though it was a little wobbly. "Good."

The cop roughly pulled me around and walked me out. I didn't miss the smug smile on Ray's fucking face. I'd soon punch it right off him.

I took one look back and saw Courtney with my phone to her ear, talking rapidly and glaring at the floor.

She believed me. That was all that mattered.

CHAPTER SEVEN

Courtney

"State, aren't you seein' your woman?"

I pushed the tingle of hearing Country call me State's woman away and said, "Country, this is State's woman. He's just been arrested by Ray Bond and has been accused of murdering someone."

"What the fuck?" he bellowed so loudly I had to pull the phone away for a moment.

"I know. It's a bunch of bullshit."

"It is, babe. Ray is a client at the brothel. He's got a hard-on for one of the girls, Lisa, and she lied to him about datin' State to get him off her back. He's been stalkin' your man, and now he goes and does this shit.

Fuck. Wreck, Death, office now. Don't you worry, babe, we'll get—"

"No, *you* don't have to worry. My father is friends with lawyers. I'm calling him now to get onto this. We'll have State out soon. I'll call when I have news."

"Courtney, you don't have to do that. We have people."

"So do I. That… that asshole interrupted our date. I'll be dealing with this and suing the hell out of him for something. I don't know what yet, but I will. I have to go."

"Courtney—"

"Talk soon." I opened my purse with jerky movements and pulled out some bills to throw onto the table before I stalked out of there. I placed State's phone in my bag and got mine out. As soon as Dad answered, I explained, "Dad, I need your help. State's been arrested for murder, but I know he didn't do it. Can you please help me get him a lawyer? Please, Dad."

"Courtney, calm down, breathe, and explain it slowly."

Once I was back in my car, I sucked in a ragged breath. My heart was beating a million miles an hour. "Okay, State and I were on our date when cops came in to arrest him. State told me before they reached us that whatever they said would be a lie. That the policeman there, a Ray Bond, had it out for him because a girl who works with State told the cop a lie that she was dating State to get this cop off her back. Obviously, it didn't work, and this cop still has it out for State. Now he's been arrested, and God knows what's happening to him." My bottom lip trembled. I quickly bit down on it.

"I need you to be honest with me, Courtney. Do you completely believe State?"

"Yes." No hesitation. No second-guessing. I knew in my heart that State was innocent.

"All right, I'll make some calls. Why don't you come over here, and we'll get to the bottom of all this mess?"

"Okay, good. Thanks, Dad. I'll leave now."

"Drive safe, princess."

"I will."

My hands shook, but I tightened them around the steering wheel. There was something wrong with that Ray Bond. But I knew it was his name and face I would need to remember because God only knew what he thought about seeing State with me on a date. If he was going to these lengths of fabricating a lie to accuse State of murder because he's obsessed with this woman, then there was a chance he'd want to keep an eye on me.

A shiver raked over me at the thought of being spied on.

No matter, since I knew my dad would be on the phone trying to get State out. Whatever evidence the police had, because they certainly had to have something to arrest him in the first place, would be faked or at least circumstantial. I could only hope the lawyer wouldn't look down on State because he was in a club and owned a brothel.

I'd done my research on Polished. From everything I learned about the place, it appeared to be aboveboard, safe, and popular. A lot of the employees had even left reviews saying how good it was to work for a place where they didn't have to worry for their safety. So surely nothing from his work could be held against him.

State would be fine.

He would be.

Unless what I saw on television was true. Could cops beat on a suspect just for fun and to get answers out of them?

If Ray was willing to take State in like he had, there was no predicting what he'd do to him.

I straightened as a thought popped into my mind. Maybe the woman this so-called cop was into would testify against Ray?

Honestly, I didn't know how things worked, but I'd bring the idea up if necessary.

I pulled into my parents' driveway and climbed out of the car with my bag clutched to my chest. State trusted me with his phone, and I wasn't about to lose it on him. Especially when I needed it to contact Country. I hoped I wasn't too rude to him before, insisting I would take care of it. They may even have a lawyer on hand, but would they be as good as Dad's contacts? I didn't want to risk it, and also, taking charge would help me stay settled until I saw State again with my own eyes.

Without knocking, I went through the front door and called, "Dad? Mom?"

"Kitchen," Mom yelled back.

I found them sitting at the dining room table. Dad had his phone in front of him. Taking a seat, I asked, "Anything?"

"Lewis has asked me to call him back when I have a bit more information."

Frustration formed in my chest. "What?"

"Where does State work? What kind of connection does this cop have with the girl?"

I nodded. "Okay. State's co-owner of Polished Pah, Pussies." My face warmed, but I pushed down the embarrassment over saying "pussies" to my father. "Um, to get a clearer picture, maybe I should have Country on speaker. He knows everything."

"Who's Country?" Mom asked.

"He's the president of the Diamond MC where State is the vice president."

"Ooh, he sounds important," Mom cooed.

"Beth, not relevant right now."

"Yes, of course. Courtney, call the president." She smiled and doubled down on her eyebrow bouncing. "I didn't realize how much I wanted to say those words until I said them." She waved me on.

I grabbed State's phone out, unlocked it, and hit Country's name.

"Court?"

"Hi, Country. I'm sitting here with my parents, and Dad's asked me a couple of things to tell the lawyer, but I wanted you to hear everything because you know more than I do."

"Got it."

"Country, this is Patty. My daughter has informed me that State is co-owner of Polished. And she also mentioned there was a girl involved from work?"

"Yeah, Patty. Her name's Lisa, and Ray Bond, the cop, is her client. He's become obsessed with her. Wants her to leave her job and marry him. She doesn't want anythin' to do with him, which is why she lied about datin' State. In the last couple of weeks, Ray has started showin' up outside the compound and a couple of times outside State's own home. He just sits and watches, but as we can all tell now, it wasn't just for kicks to try and intimidate State into leavin' Lisa. He wants to get State out of the picture, and I guess sendin' him to jail for some fucked up... shit, sorry."

Dad laughed. "It's fine, Country. Look, I'll give this information to Lewis Devlin, my lawyer friend, and see what he says. He's already found out they have a witness that places State in the area and an item they think is State's."

"This is fuckin' bullshit. Who are they sayin' he murdered? Who's tellin' the cops it was him, and what was the evidence?"

"I don't have the answers to the last two, sorry. But the victim's name is James Sullen."

We heard muttering in the background.

Country cursed. "Find out," he ordered. "Patty, you gotta know State wouldn't have murdered this guy. I swear on the club your girl is safe with my brother."

"You don't have to swear on anything, Country. My

daughter is smart. She knows who to trust, and already she's put that trust in State."

"Good to hear."

"We do have a slight problem, though."

"What's that?"

"Lewis is out of town until early tomorrow. He won't be able to get to State until then to get him out, which I'm sure he'll be able to do."

"Shit. The lawyer the club has won't be back until next week."

"State might have to stay in overnight, at least."

"No," I cried.

"I'm sorry, Courtney, but it's the best we can do. I only trust Lewis with this because he's the best with cases like these."

"Babe, don't stress for State. He can handle one night in there. I'm sure of it. Patty—hold up." Country spoke off the phone, and we couldn't hear what was being said. Then he burst out with "Tell me you're fuckin' jokin', Tech…. Christ. Patty, you let Lewis know that the victim was also a client of Lisa's."

Mom gasped, and Dad took her hand. Bile threatened as I stared wide-eyed over at my dad.

This was more serious than we'd thought.

"Country—"

"Clear the women out. We gotta have a word privately, Patty."

"Wait, I'm not leaving if it has something to do with State," I said.

"Babe, this ain't for me to tell you. State will."

"Country," I grated. "You listen here. I'm not blind. I'm not deaf or dumb. I know that being in a club can be dangerous."

"Shit, fuck. You two have been on one date, Court. *One* date."

"One date, one text message session, and a two-hour conversation. All times when I knew my heart could easily grow for that man sitting in jail because from just one sight of him, he planted a seed inside my heart and kickstarted it like no one has before."

I wasn't lying.

It may be fantastical or unbelievable, but a strong connection could be made from first sight, and it happened with State and me.

"My parents trust me, and I know with every breath, every step, every blink that I can trust State and, in turn, trust the club. Don't hide things from me. Don't think I can't take it, because I can. I will. For him, for State, I'd do anything, and you can all call me stupid or tell me it's too soon, but I know… I *know* it's not." I let out a frustrated growl and sat back in the chair. "Country, *if* you believe everything I've said and you're willing to speak to me, know I can vouch for my parents. They've shown nothing but love and support for me, my brothers, and others."

"Okay, babe," he said in the gentlest tone I'd heard from him. "Okay."

I glanced at Mom. Tears welled in her eyes as she held fingers to her lips, no doubt to stop a sob from sounding. She knew I was certain about State. She'd always told me how she and Dad had fallen in love at first sight. It might not be love yet for State, but I felt from the top of my head to the tips of my toes, we were meant to be something amazing.

"You all need to know that with the club, we protect our own in any way necessary."

I drew my brows together as I considered that the idea didn't sound bad. "I'm not sure what type of reaction you're after, Country," I confessed.

His sigh swept through the phone clearly. "By sayin' this, we're puttin' our lives in your hands, but when I say *any* way necessary, I mean that it could get dirty."

I opened my mouth to say something—I wasn't quite sure what yet—but Dad rested a hand on my arm and shook his head. He cleared his throat. "Country, maybe this conversation isn't wise to have over a phone?"

Cocking my head to the side, I thought over what Country had said, running it through my mind again and again.

Oh. *Oh.*

"You're gettin' me, Patty. But these phones are safe from prying ears. We have our guy who takes care of that. Look, this club is our family. If somethin' bad happens to one member, they have the brothers at their back. If the problem can't be dealt with in the right way, the legal way, then, and only then, do we step in. We step in to protect and make sure the problem that occurred doesn't happen again. Ever." Country let out a heavy breath. "I know this shit is deep and dark. You take your time to sort that out. Court, text me and let me know if we need to get our lawyer movin' for State. But I hoped to fuckin' Christ I haven't screwed this up for him because I know you already mean somethin' to him, and when a brother gets attached, we know it's for the long haul."

The call ended.

They hurt people to protect their own.

They probably even killed people to protect their families.

Wasn't I supposed to be scared, knowing this?

Did having this knowledge make me want to run for the hills?

No, it didn't.

"Courtney?" Dad said gently.

"Maybe it hasn't sunk it fully. But… I don't know, Dad. I should be surprised by his confession, yet…." I shrugged. "I'm not."

"Am I understanding correctly when I say that he just admitted to killing people when a problem isn't resolved?" Mom asked.

"Yes, honey," Dad said.

Mom's lips thinned as she nodded. "Well, at least we know they'd protect our daughter with the kind of ferocity that a lioness would her cub."

Dad snorted, then coughed and cleared his throat. "They've handed us their lives, as Country said. In doing so, it tells me they trust our daughter completely. I won't deny I'm afraid, but I'll stand with you, with your choice, Courtney. I know you, and I know you won't throw yourself into this relationship carelessly. If you want State in your life, even though it's only been a short amount of time, then go with what you feel is right for you. We'll always be here for you, no matter what. Still, know that we'll protect you as well, if needed."

Tears welled and fell. I turned my arm over and held his hand. "Thank you, Dad." I looked at Mom, holding my other hand out. She took it instantly with wetness in her gaze. "What do you think, Mom?"

"Well, I believe the choice is yours, sweetie."

"There's something strong growing between State and me, and it's fast." I licked my dry lips. "I also know what Country said is shocking. The whole situation is corrupt, but State has been nothing but respectful to me, and I believe he's been treated unfairly by an officer of the law. It's not right, yet that officer could get away with this. If… if he's the one who murdered that victim because of a woman *he's* obsessed with, *that's* scary. I can only hope things get sorted. One way or another."

I couldn't say it aloud, but if it meant the Diamond MC had to step in to deal with a man who would kill an innocent over an obsession, then I didn't see anything wrong with it. I didn't know if I had rose-colored goggles on for State, but I realized the club was some type of vigilante organization that righted wrongs to help the people around them.

Dad nodded. "Text Country. Tell him I'll have Lewis there in the morning."

"Thank you. Have I told you both lately what amazing parents you are?"

"Not for a while, but I know." Mom smiled.

They were really the best. Not every parent could sit by and let their daughter date someone who was in a club, knowing they didn't always operate inside of the law.

I hoped I hadn't broken their trust with my decision, but I highly doubt I could.

State would be in my life. Especially if I did kidnap the man in order to protect him.

CHAPTER EIGHT

State

The cops had known their evidence was circumstantial at best. It hadn't been enough to get a murder charge to stick, so Ray Bond had booked me for a couple of bogus traffic offenses and told me I'd have to stay overnight since my lawyer couldn't make it until today.

I'd hated staying in a goddamn holding cell, mainly because Courtney would be going out of her mind. Christ, I'd never prayed before, but I did yesterday, wanting my little mouse to believe me. Country had better set her straight when it came to Lisa.

While I hadn't known the lawyer the club had brought in, but fuck me, he was a genius. As soon as he'd entered the station this morning, he had the cops stumbling over their asses, and even reamed them out about the traffic charges.

I was hella relieved, especially as it meant I was getting out of here.

"Dominic," Lewis, my kickass lawyer, said, dragging me from my thoughts when we reached the foyer of the station.

"State, man," I corrected.

He nodded. "State. Here." He held out a phone to me. "Your president asked me to get you to call him before we went outside."

Confusion had me tensing. "Right." I typed in Country's number and put it to my ear.

"State?"

"Brother."

"Fuck, brother, it's good to hear your voice." I could hear the smile in his tone.

"That smug bastard—"

His tone quickly switched when he read how pissed off I was. "I know. I fuckin' know. He'll be dealt with. Look, there's shit you gotta know."

"What?" I clipped.

"Court—"

"Is she all right? Did she ring you? Does she know it's all a goddamn lie? That I'd been set up?"

"If you shut up a sec, I'll tell you." Country chuckled. "You gotta put a ring on her finger, brother."

I stared down at the floor. "Huh?"

"Brother, Court rang me and *told* me she was gonna

deal with the situation when I'd tried to say we had a lawyer. The guy standin' with you is her dad's friend. She went to her parents straightaway and got the help you needed. Just sucked he couldn't get there until this mornin'. Our lawyer is outta town for the week, so it's lucky you met your woman and that she was beyond pissed, so she sorted this shit out."

Not only did my little mouse believe me, but she had my back.

Christ, that meant the world. Even though I was tired as fuck, energy zapped through me.

"I'm gonna put a ring on her finger," I told my brother as I nodded to myself.

Country chuckled. "That ain't all."

"Tell me."

"Brother, I was on speaker with her 'rents because Patty—her dad—wanted all the info he could get for the lawyer and…. Now, don't be pissed, but I was straight with them. They know how our club runs. They know we'd do anythin' to protect our people, and they understood the meanin' to *anythin'*."

I sucked in a sharp breath and bit out, "Country—"

"No, listen. I gave them time to let it sink in, told Court to text me *if* she was still gonna help after havin' that news."

"And? Don't leave me hangin', brother."

"State, clue in, brother. Her dad's lawyer is standin' with you. He wouldn't be if they didn't accept our ways. She's gold, brother. Pure fuckin' gold, and hell, so's her family. You lucky son of a bitch."

She was mine.

My little mouse was meant to be.

This was the reason why I'd felt that sharp connection from the first moment my gaze had landed on her shy form.

She was made for me.

I'd never felt so light in my chest before, but fuck me, she made it happen.

I could only hope I didn't scare her off with how goddamn intense my world was, but knowing she had my back, understood my world, and accepted me had given me a good feeling she wouldn't run.

"Let the brothers know she's off-limits. She's mine."

He snorted. "Like they didn't know already from that night at the compound. But I'll tell them anyway."

"Gotta go. We'll talk soon."

"Yeah, brother. Got some other information about that fucker, but thought you'd want to know this more."

"Damn right. Thanks, brother."

"Anythin' for a brother," he stated and then ended the call. When I turned to the lawyer, he held out my wallet and keys.

"I collected these for you."

"Thanks." We switched items, and I said, "Look, how much does the club owe you?"

"Nothing."

"What? If Court's family paid for this—"

His hand shot up. "They didn't. Patty knew to call me with this type of situation because I've shared with him in the past that I have a son in a motorcycle club in

Australia. The Hawks MC. I know how their club runs, and from the information Patty gave me, it's very similar to yours." His jaw clenched. "Some people get away with too much, but I believe they'll get what's coming to them." He handed me a card. "My son would be annoyed if I didn't offer my help. Anytime the Diamond MC needs assistance, please don't hesitate."

I blinked down at the card. This day was filled with one surprise after another. "You're fuckin' with me?"

He smirked. "Not at all." He waved the card a little.

"What's your son's name in the club?"

Lewis actually blushed. "It's Muff."

Chuckling, I reached out and took the card, placing it in my wallet before I pocketed it. "Let your boy and his club know that if they ever need help in the US, we'd be happy to step in."

He tipped his head down. "Thank you, I will." We started for the door.

"Seriously, Lewis. I appreciate you steppin' up today. The offer to help not only goes to your boy. You need anythin', just call us. You got Country's number now."

"Yes, and thank you again. I'll keep that in mind."

"Good." As soon as we stepped outside, I spotted Courtney at the bottom of the steps, standing between an older version of herself and a man. She had her fingers pressed against her mouth and shifted from one foot to the other.

My woman had been worried for me.

Blood coursed through my veins as my heart tried to jump out of my chest at the sight of her. It felt like I flew down those steps, because in the next blink, she was in front of me as I slid one hand around her waist and the other through her fucking amazing thick hair, tugging her close.

"Fuck, little mouse," I growled just before I took her mouth and claimed it as my own in a hard, rough, but damn hot kiss. She gripped my tee at my gut and held on while she gave back as good as I delivered.

It was the kiss that sealed the deal. I'd never had my pulse tripping, my gut spinning, and my heart beating near out of my chest when I'd kissed anyone else.

Just her.

My perfect little mouse.

A throat cleared, and I cursed myself silently for probably fucking up meeting her parents for the first time. But as soon as I'd seen her, I'd had to have my first taste.

Breaking the kiss with a last gentle one, I stared down at my woman. "Hey, baby."

"State."

"No, little mouse. Not State. Dominic for you and only you."

"Dominic," she whispered.

My cock jerked. "Yeah, angel."

"You're okay?"

"More than okay. The woman I'm into had my back and got me help. It means a fuckin' lot to me, Court."

She smiled. "I think I got that message."

Grinning, I tucked her under my arm and faced her

parents with my hand held out to her dad. "Patty, I'm State."

He took my hand and shook. It was good to see his lips tipped up and not frowning. "State, nice to meet you. Sorry it's under these circumstances."

"Me too." I nodded and glanced at the older image of Court.

"This is my wife, Beth."

I tipped my chin up. "Beth."

She gaped a little as she looked from me to her daughter and back again. "Do you like babies?"

"Mom!" Courtney cried.

Laughing, I hugged her into my side tighter. "Yeah, Beth. I like babies."

"Okay then."

"Lewis, thank you again," Patty said, and I shifted the two of us back to add my lawyer into the huddle.

"Anytime, Patty. But you still owe me a card night."

"I'll make sure it's soon."

Lewis nodded and took my outstretched hand. "Thanks again, Lewis."

"You're welcome. I'll leave you all to it. Have a good day." We watched in silence as he walked off.

"You'll have to come to dinner this Sunday night," Beth said, facing us as Patty put his arm around her.

"I'd like that, thanks."

Court groaned. "Can we make sure the three stooges aren't there?"

"It's called family dinner night for a reason, honey." Beth smiled.

I kissed the top of Courtney's head. "It's all good, babe. I can handle them."

Lifting her gaze, she warned, "Just remember you said that."

"I will. You're stuck with me now."

"Okay," she said softly, curling her arms around my waist.

Turning to her parents, I asked, "You mind givin' me a lift to the compound?"

Patty flicked his gaze to his daughter. "Actually, you're in the hands of our daughter. She brought her own car to go and get your vehicle at the restaurant."

"Sounds good. It was great to meet you both," I told them.

"You too, son." Patty nodded while Beth smiled warmly.

No wonder my little mouse was damn perfect; she'd come from good people. Not many would meet me, take in my tats, how I talk, my job, my life, and not even blink about it. It blew my damn mind they were entrusting me with their daughter.

"I'll make sure she gets home safe."

Patty locked eyes with me for a moment. "We know, State." Maybe I was reading into those words, but to me, they said he accepted me into their life.

Christ, maybe I was just tired and thinking too much.

With a final goodbye, I waited until they were in their car and taking off before I pulled Court around and wound my arms around her shoulders. "Like your 'rents, baby."

"I'm glad."

"Lookin' forward to dinner night."

Her gaze narrowed. "I swear if my brothers—"

Chuckling, I kissed her rant away, and she melted into me, taking what I gave her like she was made to do it.

"Let's get outta here," I said against her lips.

"Please."

As we made our way to her car, a feeling of being watched crawled over my skin. I glanced back.

Ray fucking Bond stood at the top of the stairs, glaring down at me.

I smirked and shot him a two-finger wave.

Yeah, fucker, you'll soon get what's coming to you.

CHAPTER NINE

Courtney

"*N*o, little mouse. Not State. Dominic for you and only you."

Dominic.

Dominic.

Dominic.

He'd asked me to use his name instead of a club name, and being so used to State in my head, I repeated it over and over so I didn't mess up. Though, every time I thought of using his name on the drive to collect his car, my belly tingled with excitement.

When I pulled up beside his vehicle, he turned to me. "Follow me to the compound, yeah?"

"Yes, Dominic." The reaction I got from him by

using his name was instant. He grinned, gripped the back of my head, and dragged me close to kiss me.

Each kiss was like a ride that got your blood pumping, your body waking, and your heart racing.

He was going to get me addicted.

The kiss tapered off into small pecks and left me breathing heavily. Someone laid on the horn behind me, since I was double-parked. Dominic looked out the back window and growled under his breath—actually growled. I would never admit how my pussy pulsed at the sound.

Shaking my head, I smiled. "Go. I'll follow you there."

He kissed me again quickly and climbed out of the car. Through the rearview mirror, I watched the impatient driver behind me immediately wind up his window when he saw Dominic, causing me to laugh.

Sure, the man held an edge of danger, and I was certain he looked intimidating to the average passerby. But not to me. The rough tone in his voice called to my ears. His sweet smirks, satisfied grins, and beaming smiles took my breath each time. His ink was a work of art, one I would paint if I could get it right. And his eyes, they were dark pools of endless wants, desires, happiness, angers, knowledge, and so much more.

Everything about him touched my heart, mind, body, and soul.

As soon as I was following Dominic in my car, I reminded myself this was real. Not only the connection and the whirlwind of us, but that Dominic was out of jail, and he was all right.

But what would the officer's next move be?

Not knowing had tension bubbling in my belly. Those bubbles could too easily build and develop into a tsunami threatening to take me under.

Only my belief in Dominic and his brothers in the Diamond MC kept me breathing through the rising tide of anxiety. They would work this out. I wasn't sure I wanted to know exactly how.

Except I couldn't stop reminding myself that this cop, who was supposed to uphold the law, was stalking Dominic, obsessed with a woman, and had possibly killed someone over her. He'd gone too far, and honestly, he deserved whatever retribution the club delivered. I just didn't need to know the details.

Once I was parked beside Dominic, I climbed out and met him at the back of my car. He stepped into my path and cupped my cheeks, bringing my gaze up to his.

His dark eyes ran over my face as he smiled softly.

"What's wrong?" I asked.

He shook his head. "Nothin' at all. Only wonderin' how I got so goddamn lucky to have you step up for me."

Aiming for nonchalance, I shrugged. "He interrupted our date."

Dominic threw his head back and laughed as he wrapped me up into a tight hug. I held on, my lips twitching, and enjoyed the show, glad to see him laughing after dealing with a stalker cop.

When he kissed my temple, a contented sigh fell from my lips.

Yes, I really wanted this to stick. I wanted there to be an us for a very long time. Maybe it sounded crazy, since it had been such a short amount of time, but I wasn't going to push him away and let my fear of this failing take over.

I was going to cling.

And boy, did I have something to cling to.

Dominic curled an arm around my shoulders and led us into the compound. "How many kids do you want?"

It was lucky he had a hold of me because I tripped on nothing and nearly fell. Of course, he started chuckling.

Shock had me sucking in a breath, only to choke on it. I coughed out, "Isn't it too soon to talk about that?"

Chuckling, he pressed his lips to my temple. "I figured your mom might ask when I come to family dinner night."

Sighing at the reminder, I still grinned as I pressed my face into his chest, which was still shaking with mirth. "I can't believe she said that."

"It was cute."

I snorted. "It wasn't."

"For a while, it's only been me and the brothers. Yeah, we have our family nights, but I've had no one at my side at them. I have no extended family whose houses I can go to dinner at. So really, I'll take all the pestering in the world because it means she cares. It means she's accepted me in your life."

Emotion caught in my throat, and I tightened my arms around him. "Okay, Dominic."

He tipped my head back with a fisted hand in my hair. "Fuckin' love hearin' my name come from your lips. But, baby, I'm gonna love it more when I get the chance to be inside you, and you say it then."

The sudden reaction in my body from his words, honest words that I had never heard spoken to me like that before, was a big spike of adrenaline. A shiver raked over me as my belly tingled and nipples hardened.

"I ain't sayin' it needs to be soon. I'm fine with waitin', little mouse, because I know you're worth it."

"Dominic," I breathed.

"Yeah, just like that, all breathy and shit. Gonna fuckin' love it."

"Soon."

His lips twitched. "What's soon?"

"You and me in bed, please."

"Anythin' you want. You just tell me when."

"When."

He chuckled again, but I wasn't joking. Heck, I wanted him in all the ways I could. Under me, over me, behind me—all of it.

"Let's go see the brothers first, and you have a think about it when you're not horny."

"Your fault. You get me all hot and bothered and stuff."

He pressed his mouth against mine. Once there, he said, "Glad to know I can turn you on like you do me."

I pulled back, eyes flaring. "I do?"

He gripped my butt and dragged my lower body forward to press his erection against me.

Dear God, he was hard, so very hard. I wanted to cover him with my hand, yet drop to my knees at the same time. This man turned me into an insatiable woman even before we'd had a chance to do anything. How would I be after the deed?

"Yeah, little mouse, you do." Smirking, he shook his head, turned me, and gently ushered me forward while chuckling as he said, "Askin' me if she turns me on. Jesus, babe."

"Well, I didn't know."

He hooked an arm around my neck as we continued to walk. It was a little awkward, bumping into each other, but I liked how he wanted me close. Wanted to walk into the clubhouse with me under his arm in front of everyone he classed as family. The action gave me a boost in confidence, but it also left me soft and gooey on the inside.

He kissed the side of my neck. "Now you do."

When we stepped into the common room, a roar of clapping and greetings reached us. Dominic held me to his side while he spoke with his brothers and they gave him one-armed hugs or chin lifts.

Country stepped forward and placed a hand on my head, ruffling my hair. He looked at Dominic. "You're gonna need help with this one. I couldn't getta word in edgewise when she was in a moment."

Mock glaring, I rolled my eyes. "I wasn't that bad."

"Tech," Country boomed, and in the next second, I heard my voice over a PA system. *"Country, this is State's woman. He's just been arrested by Ray Bond and has been accused of murdering someone."*

"What the fuck?" was broadcast next in Country's voice.

"I know. It's a bunch of bullshit. My father is friends with lawyers. I'm calling him now to get onto this. We'll have State out soon. I'll call when I have news." I was sure Country said something in between that, but it had been cut out.

"Courtney, you don't have to do that. We have people."

"So do I. That... that asshole interrupted our date. I'll be dealing with this and suing the hell out of him for something. I don't know what yet, but I will. I have to go."

"Courtney—"

"Talk soon." The call ended.

Cheers erupted, but I ignored them when Dominic pulled me around to face him. The heat to his eyes could have burned me, but in the best way. "Fuck me," he clipped in a low, rough tone. He shook his head.

"Let's break it up, brothers. They're gonna have a moment," someone yelled, and I heard them scatter.

I shrugged and rolled my eyes, trying to compose myself. When they landed back on Dominic, I said, "It's not a big deal."

His gaze darkened even more. He took my hand and

led me out of the room. I didn't miss the catcalls, though I ignored them. If he was that taken by my actions, I wasn't going to argue, especially if we were headed to a bedroom and I was going to get myself some.

Our steps ate up the floor, and Dominic kept glancing at me, both of us smiling sweetly at each other. When we reached his bedroom, he tugged me through the door and closed it, pushing me up against the wall beside it.

"I mean, some parts Country said were left out." Why was I even bothering talking?

His hands slapped to the wall on each side of my head. "You're my woman?"

"Country said it first, but that part wasn't in there."

"Are you my woman?"

"Dominic."

"Courtney."

I licked my suddenly dry lips, watching him follow the movement. "I would like to be."

He groaned and dipped to rest his forehead against mine. "Good, baby, because I wanna be your man."

I gasped. I couldn't help it. I uttered, "You do?"

"Yeah, little mouse. Know it's soon, also know we have a lot of gettin' to know each other, but fuck, babe, you were meant to be mine when you walked into the compound. I knew it then, and I definitely know it now."

"Okay." His gaze flared at my acceptance, warming me in a way that made me want to curl up under his attention.

"We're gonna see where this goes, but I've got an idea it's gonna be good things for us, little mouse."

"So do I." And I did, right down to my bone marrow.

He grinned. "Glad we're on the same page." He dropped his chin to kiss my nose, and then straightened.

When he made a move to open the door, I asked, "That's it?"

"What you mean?"

"You're just going to go back out there?"

"I was, but is my woman wantin' to do somethin' else?"

"Yes. Me. Do me." The need in my voice was evident, but I didn't care. Not when I was so close to having him.

He wore the widest grin I had seen on him yet when he spun me into his arms and twirled, yes twirled, me around until we were close to the bed.

"Baby, you gotta know the brothers have a good idea what we're doin' in here."

My face heated. "I know... but I've pushed that to the back of my mind because right now, all I can think about is you."

He wound his arms around me tightly. "Jesus, baby." He cupped my cheeks and bent a little to have my eyes. "Little mouse, I need to make sure you're okay with stayin' in here for the next activity while the brothers are out there knowin' we're about to fuck."

"Oh," I drew out. "Then yes, I'm okay with them knowing. I mean, everyone has sex. We definitely won't be the first ones in this compound to have done it with other people in the building."

God, I loved his smile.

"That's true, babe." He straightened. "Can we put this on hold until I have a shower?"

Of course he would want one; he'd been in jail all night. He could even want something to eat or need sleep or anything else other than sex.

With one hand, he gently pinched my cheeks together with his thumb on one side and fingers on the other while he pushed my face up to meet his gaze.

"Can see you thinkin'. I don't need anythin' else, just a shower. The only mess I want on you is my own."

Well...

"Um, I could have one with you?" A squeal escaped me when he picked me up and threw me over his shoulder.

He picked me up like it was nothing. Then again, it probably was, since he was tall and huge.

We really did fit well together.

CHAPTER TEN

State

My hard cock throbbed under my jeans, as eager as I was to get inside my woman. Christ, I could still hear in my head what she'd said to Country. She'd called herself my woman. She'd shut him down to take control and get me out.

"Your dress is pretty, baby, but it'd look better on the floor."

She dragged her top teeth over her plump bottom lip and boldly lifted her arms.

Fuck yes.

I ran my hands slowly down over her waist, her hips, and her thighs. When I stopped at the hem of her dress, I took it in my hands and met her gaze. A quiet mewl left her lips.

Yeah, she wanted this.

Leaning in, I kissed the top of the breast peeking out of her dress, and then straightened as I pulled it up and off.

Jesus Christ.

I ran my gaze over her slowly and groaned. "Fuck, you're gorgeous."

"Shut up."

I blinked. "What?"

She waved me off. "You don't have to say that kind of thing. I'm a done deal."

Scrunching my brows down, I lifted my upper lip in a silent snarl. "Who the fuck messed with your head?" I dragged her close with my hand on the back of her head. "Whoever said you weren't gorgeous, I'll fuckin' deal with. Baby, I don't talk shit. I say what I say because I mean it. You're goddamn stunnin', and I won't have you thinkin' any different or brushin' my comments off."

Her hands on my chest tightened, and a sexy pink coated her cheeks. It was her breathy response that had my dick pulsing, though. "Okay, Dominic. I-I didn't mean it, honestly. My words are a knee-jerk reaction, something I'm used to doing, but I promise to try and curb it because I do believe you when *you* say it."

"Good. Because I fuckin' love what I see every damn time I look at you."

She lifted onto her tiptoes and pressed her lips

against mine. Before I could chase the kiss for something deeper, she eased back. "Thank you, hon."

I grunted, still annoyed with whoever the hell had treated my woman wrong and gave her insecurities. The best thing I could do was show her how much I loved her body.

She laughed and kissed my chest. "Stop being butthurt. I told you I believe you." She rocked against me. "The evidence is right behind these jeans."

"Did you just tell me to stop being butthurt?"

She flashed me a smile. "I did."

Snorting, I bent and nipped at her shoulder. "I'll try and stop, as long as you don't say shit like that again or wave me off."

"All right, Dom. You can fight my insecurities for me."

Dom. I liked it.

Threading my fingers through her hair, I tugged until she arched her neck for me. "Damn right I will. And I'll win every fuckin' time." I kissed her pulse, bit at the lobe of her ear, and trailed my tongue over her skin. Her hands slid to my waist and gripped, fingers clenching and a slight vibration pulsing through her body.

"Dom, please."

Shit, I had to get her in the shower.

Unable to resist, I sucked on her skin where her shoulder met her neck, drawing out a needy moan from her.

"Shower. Now." She half-heartedly pushed at my gut, the amusement in her voice loud and clear.

I kissed the place where I left my mark and straightened, looking at it.

"Yes, yes, you're very proud of yourself."

Chuckling, I nodded. "I am."

She smiled and cupped my cock, making a harsh breath leave my lips. "Good. Now start the shower and get some clothes off, please."

"Anythin'." I dragged my tee over my head and dropped it to the floor, then undid my jeans as I kicked off my boots. I pushed my jeans, boxers, and socks down and off. When I lifted my gaze, I zeroed in on her parted lips, acutely aware of her heaving chest and the hand she held over her heart.

"You're a work of art." Wonder shone in her eyes. She stepped close and ran her hands over my shoulders, my pecs, my stomach. Each touch left a trail of goose bumps. "So many tattoos and muscles."

I fought hard not to preen like a damn peacock. "Glad you like them, little mouse." I pressed a kiss to her temple and shifted over to the shower. Opening the door, I started the water, feeling her gaze on me before she slid her hands over my back.

Christ, she was driving me crazy.

"Bra and panties, baby," I ordered roughly, fixing the water to the right temperature. I stepped under the spray and faced her, brushing my hair from my face to see the show of her removing the rest of her clothes.

Fucking grateful she didn't hide her body from me.

Her tits bounced a little when she dropped the bra. Her pussy was neatly trimmed short, and the need to put my face between her legs for a taste spurred me on.

"Get in here," I clipped.

She bit her bottom lip and moved into the shower, closing the door behind her. I took her hand and pulled her close, cupping her cheeks. I shifted out from under the warm water to capture her lips in a deep, wet kiss.

She wound her arms around my waist and gripped my ass. The movement easy and feeling so damn right, I thrust against her. With my cock rubbing against her belly, precum leaked and left a silky trail on her soft skin as our kiss continued.

Court's mouth ate at my own—all teeth, tongues, lips. It was like she was made just for me. Kissed me how I liked it. Needy, raw, and passionate. Hot one second, soft and gentle the next.

Christ.

We only broke apart to breathe, and then my woman was grabbing the soap to wash me. I watched her, my chest expanding with warm emotions. Reaching out, I played with her heavy tits as she kept working the soap over me. I pinched her nipples, earning me a gasp and bite to my chest.

Not one to be left out of doing the teasing, she soaped up her hand and, with a cheeky smirk, washed over my junk, tugging on my balls and curling her fingers through my pubes.

"Fuck, baby." I wound her hair in my hand and gripped the strands. I watched her staring at her hand as she wrapped it around my cock and jerked up and down.

Drawing her in closer, I slid my free hand between her legs and found she wasn't only wet from the water.

"Dom," she moaned, spreading her legs more for me. I dipped a finger inside and drew it up to circle her clit. "Please."

"What, little mouse? What do you need?" When she didn't say anything as I dipped inside her again, I went on, "You want my cock? It's gonna fit so goddamn well in this pussy."

She crashed her forehead into my chest, panting. I cupped the back of her neck, rubbing my thumb over the side of her soft skin. "Fuck, I can't wait to feel your heat. To have it surrounding me."

She whimpered.

"Yeah, baby, this pussy is all for me. All mine."

Reacting to my words, she tightened her grip on my cock. I hissed out a breath. If she wasn't careful, I'd come all over her belly and feet.

Shit, that was not gonna happen.

I slipped my fingers free, and she let out a sound of protest. "Baby, I gotta get inside you before I lose it." I took her shoulders, shifted her to the side, and fucking rushed out of the shower to grab a condom. I was back in seconds, closing the door and seeing her leaning against the cool tiles, watching me as she ran her hands over her gorgeous tits.

"Dom, hurry."

The neediness in her words shot to my balls. I tore

the condom open with my teeth and sheathed my cock in the rubber. I stalked over to her, picked her up, and kissed her.

The hunger I had for this woman was intense.

She wrapped her legs around me, her fingers on my shoulders digging in. Like she wanted to bury herself inside me by digging. *Christ.*

My cock brushed over her pussy, easily gliding from her wetness as I rocked against her.

"Dom," she pleaded, tightening her hold around my neck. I lifted her a little more, reached between us, and lined myself up. When she nodded, I slowly pushed inside. Her eyes closed, and she dropped her head back, moaning until I was all the way in.

I rested there, kissing her neck, biting, sucking. She clamped around me, squeezing my cock tight. "Fuck," I clipped. "I gotta move."

She lifted her head and nodded. "Yes."

Withdrawing, I watched her bite her bottom lip as her face softened and a satisfied smile broke free. When I thrust back in, she moaned and dropped her mouth to my neck, sucking.

My hands dug into her ass cheeks when I pulled back out, then in. Her tightness had me goddamn losing my mind.

"Mouth," I growled.

She rewrapped her arms around my neck, lifted her head, and gave me what I wanted. We kissed, her tongue tangling with mine, our lips moving in sync.

Fucking perfect.

I pushed my pelvis against her harder, tipping her ass up more to press into her mound, against her clit. She whimpered into my mouth, and I drank it down. I wanted every sound, every whimper and moan.

Court broke the kiss, panting. I bit at her chin, licked over her jaw, and sucked her earlobe into my mouth, tonguing it.

"Dom, God, yes, please. I'm close."

With renewed focus, I pressed her into the wall, stuffed my face into her neck, and drilled in and out of her. Her tightness suffocated my cock, drawing my balls up.

"Jesus, baby. Fuck."

"Yes, Dom. Just… there." Her nails raked over my back, and her pussy gripped, released, and gripped over and over.

Lost.

I was completely lost in the feeling.

My load filled the condom as I groaned into her slick skin. I pumped in and out until I was drained.

"Christ," I uttered.

"Hmm" was Courtney's reply, and then she giggled a little.

Lifting my head, I quirked my brow. "What the hell you laughin' for?" When she laughed again, her pussy squeezed me, causing me to shudder. I had to withdraw from her heat.

"Of course you couldn't be bad at something."

I jerked my head back, shocked. "You wanted me to be bad?"

She blushed. "Well, no. But I just can't believe how perfect you are."

She thought I was perfect?

She was wrong.

It was her.

All her.

I brushed her wet hair from her face. "I'm far from it, little mouse. Though I'm happy you think so." With a kiss, I turned from her to get rid of the condom. I opened the door and threw it into the bin near the basin. Facing her, I dragged her under the spray of water again.

"What are you doing?" she asked.

"Gotta wash you like you did me, and then we're gonna hit the bed so I can finally get a taste of that sweet pussy."

"Dom," she breathed as I ran my hand over her mound.

"Yeah, little mouse, that's how you sounded with my cock in you."

She dropped her head to my chest and let me play while I used my free hand to run the soap over her tits. "We're going to run out of warm water."

"I'll keep you warm and we won't be in here long. Want you on the bed spread out for me."

"I-I can't come again."

"You can, Court, and I'll show you how."

She didn't deny me. She let me have my fun.

And I fucking did.

CHAPTER ELEVEN

State

I'd left Court sleeping in my bed. I woke not that long ago with my gut rumbling. I needed food and to take some back to my woman as well. A smile tugged at my lips. The images of my little mouse would live in the forefront of my mind.

I wanted my hands on her again.

I wanted my mouth between her legs, drinking down her juices.

My cock jerked.

Christ, I'd never get enough. I made my way into the kitchen, and the chatter stopped. Country, Death, and Quake stood at the counter, eating pizza and grinning over at me.

"Not a word," I ordered.

Country's hands rose. "Wouldn't think of it. Not when we know she's a keeper."

Death nodded. "If you don't—"

"She's mine."

The fuckers chuckled.

Quake made his way over and patted my shoulder. "Happy for you, brother."

I tipped my chin up. "Thanks." He nodded before leaving, munching on his slice of pepperoni. When my gut growled again, I grabbed a couple of plates and put some slices on them. "Dusty been cookin' again?"

Country thinned his lips. "Yeah."

Death rolled his eyes. "No matter how many times you tell her she doesn't have to, you know she will."

I swallowed my bite. "She thinks it's her way to make up for stayin' here."

If Country's glares could kill me, I'd be dead. "She doesn't have to."

Death gripped his shoulder. "We know." He rolled his eyes. "How about we give State the good news?"

Country brightened, pushing any thought of Dusty away. "You got time to chat?"

"Let me leave some pizza for Court, and I'll meet you in the office."

"You got it," Country replied.

On my way out, I grabbed two sodas out of the refrigerator and pushed them into my back pockets. The common room was quiet. A few club girls lingered around the brothers who were either off work or on break, and there was one prospect manning the bar. At least I wouldn't get caught up in conversation when I wanted to know what the good news was that Country and Death had.

In my room, I shut the door as Court rolled over in the bed. I held up the plate. "Pizza."

Her smile warmed my chest and gripped my gut.

Jesus, she looked good in my bed, naked with the sheet pulled up under her arms.

I placed the plate on the bedside table with the drinks and sat in the crook of her hip. Brushing stray strands of hair from her face, I leaned in and kissed her temple, cheeks, and nose. She tipped her head up to give me her lips, and I made the most of it.

Pulling back, I grinned down at her. "Like you here. Like knowin' you're in here. Wanna see you in my bed at my house, though."

"Okay," she whispered.

"Okay," I mimicked just as softly. "You all right if I duck out and talk to the brothers for a bit?"

She nodded. "You brought me pizza. I'll be fine."

Chuckling, I asked, "That all I gotta do to please you? Bring you food after a round of hot-as-fuck sex?"

"Well…" She pushed herself up and leaned against the headboard. The sheet slipped down, showing me her gorgeous tits. Too quickly, she pulled the cover up to tuck under her arms. "Probably," she admitted with a smile.

"Deal." I went to kiss her again, but she palmed my face and shoved me back, picking up her pizza. "Evil."

"You wore me out, Dom. Hungry." I'd believe it if she'd grabbed her slice and bit into it, but her gaze was locked onto my mouth.

"You're full of shit."

She nodded. "I am. Kiss me, please."

"You got it, little mouse."

When I opened the door to Country's office, he and Death started clapping. "We thought we'd lost you, brother."

Shaking my head, I ignored their taunts because I was too fucking happy. I took the seat next to Death and opposite Country's desk. "You gonna give me this good news or what?"

Country straightened, locking his fingers together to rest on the desk. "Ray Bond."

"It'd better be the best fuckin' news by tellin' me the motherfucker got hit by a car or somethin'."

"A car will be involved," Death said.

"Give it to me straight, brothers, please."

"Tech was all over shit last night while you were in jail. He's got the proof that Ray killed that victim he was tryin' to pin on you. The dickhead kept the knife, the victim's wallet, and bloody clothes in his car that Torch searched last night."

"You're messin'?"

"We're not," Death replied, grinning. "He's that much of a dumb fuck."

"More good news. Ray decided to pay Lisa a visit after you got out of jail. The brothers picked him and his car up. He's in the basement."

I stood as my heart slammed into my chest. I clenched and unclenched my hands again and again.

The brothers chuckled, and Country held a hand up. "Hold your jets, brother."

Grinding my teeth together, I sat back down.

"We have a plan," he continued. "You know we won't let him get away with fuckin' with you and killin' an innocent. He deserves everythin' he gets. But we also need to be careful. You can't be involved."

"What the fuck?"

"Brother, listen. He arrested you, and with what we have planned, he's gonna try and pin this on the club, but mostly on you. You need a full cover, people to back up where you were. Stick with your woman. Take her out, be seen in public. I know this is a shit deal, but it's to keep you out of jail."

I hated this deal. Knowing I wouldn't be able to get my hands on the cunt had my blood boiling. "What's the plan with him?"

"Tech, the smart prick, came up with the idea." Death grinned. "We've got his car stashed at his place. He frequents a bar down the road from his house. Boom, who is a similar size and height and kind of looks like him, is gonna stumble in there actin' drunk, and he'll be wearin' the change of clothes and hat we found in his car. He won't stay long, and because the barman is a friend, he knows to kick him right back out. But it's proof he went in there smashed."

"Where's this goin'?"

Country grinned. "Ray's gonna get in his car and have a car accident. When the cops arrive, he'll smell like a brewery. They'll search the car, find the evidence, and he'll be arrested."

It sounded like a good plan. "But what happens if they don't search the car?"

"Hell, we'll leave the trunk open so they'll look in there," Death said.

"He'll rant and rave that this was all us, but he won't have anythin' to stick. Not when he's drunk off his ass from the alcohol we'll poor down his throat. They'll think he's got it out for us after arresting you. It'll work," Country stated.

"Who's crashin' the car?"

They both looked at me.

Snorting, I shook my head. "Torch."

"Yeah, the brother's excited about it."

Not only was Torch an adrenaline junkie, but he got a little crazy when it came to protecting the club.

"Brother, I've got faith. I just fuckin' hate sittin' back and not bein' involved."

They both grinned. "The best part we haven't told you is, good old Ray needs to be knocked around a little to make it look like it was him who crashed the car."

Adrenaline pumped through my veins, and I grinned back. "Let's get this show on the road then."

Down in the basement, I found Ray sitting on a

chair, not tied, not bound, just sitting there glaring at the brothers who surrounded him. Quake, Tech, Wreck, and Torch. What probably kept him staying put was the way Torch was dancing around him with his blowtorch in his hand.

"Reason number twenty this tool is good to burn people with." Torch leaned into him. "I like the way my victims squeal and plead, but they know they fucked with the wrong people, and there ain't no escape."

Torch spotted us, straightened, and started cackling. "Looks like the party's about to start." He bounced over to the wall of tools and placed the blowtorch back where it belonged, turning with a clap of his hands.

Ray's gaze locked on Country and me while Death slipped further into the room. "Do you know how much trouble you'll all be in? I'm a police officer. You're all going to rot in jail."

Country nodded to Death where he stood behind Ray. Death leaned over him and pinched Ray's jaw to open it just as Wreck and Torch grabbed his arms, holding him down.

Quake moved in front of Ray and helped Death pry his mouth open. Death poured some bourbon down and stepped back. Ray coughed and sputtered, spilling it down over the front of himself.

"You can't do this,' he rasped and coughed again.

Chuckling, I stepped closer. "You'll soon realize, Ray, that we can do fuckin' anythin'."

"Tech?" Country called.

Tech moved over to the counter and picked up an

iPad. "We've got an hour to play and get him out to the spot."

"Plenty of time." I nodded.

They held Ray down again and poured more liquid down his throat.

He thought being a cop made him invincible.

He thought he could mess with me. Mess with the club.

He thought he could kill someone and get away with it.

He would slowly work out he couldn't, and by the end of the day, he'd know it for sure.

"Enough for now. I want him coherent."

Ray stopped coughing and looked up at me. "She'll never be yours—"

Laughing, I shook my head. "You dumb fuck, she was never mine in the first place. She only told you I was hers to get you off her back."

"No, she wouldn't."

"You killed an innocent for someone who acted like she was into you… because it was her fucking job. You let your obsession fuck up your life, and you chose wrong when you came after me and my brothers. Now you'll know. Now you'll learn. And pay."

My fist connected to his cheek, then his gut and jaw.

What sucked was that by the time we were done with him, he was too drunk to even feel the pain. Still, it was worth it, and he could rot in jail for all I cared. Though, from what Tech told me, we weren't the only ones Ray had fucked over, and he'd soon get to see the others he'd screwed over when he got put behind bars.

Later, outside my bedroom door, I paused and looked down at myself. There were a couple of blood splatters on me, and I couldn't help but worry what my little mouse would think when I told her what I'd done. I'd made sure to check with Country that I could inform her. He gave me the go-ahead right away, knowing I saw the two of us staying strong, and she'd already proved herself. I also wanted to be honest with her, wanted her to know my real world and see how she'd deal with it.

A small amount of worry still gripped my chest and had my gut clenching.

Could I lose my chance at something good?

Would she walk away?

Country had said Court knew what our world was like, but in reality, with it right in her face, she could change her mind about me.

Fuck me. I didn't want that to happen. If she ran, I'd chase her. I get her to understand somehow.

My hand actually shook when I twisted the door handle and pushed it open.

The smile that greeted me died.

She'd been sitting in my bed wearing my tee, but as soon as she saw me, she threw the blankets back and stood in front of me. Her hands fluttered out, only to stop and draw back in to press against her stomach.

"Is it your blood?"

"No, Court."

Her brows pinched, her gaze slowly raking over me. She thinned her lips before blowing out a breath. "Are you able to tell me who?"

"The cop" was all I supplied as fear sliced at my insides.

She'll run.

She'll leave you.

She won't like your world.

She's too good for here.

She's too good for you.

"Ray Bond?"

I nodded.

"Dominic, what happened?"

Unlocking my jaw, I told her, "The brothers had him in the basement. Torch searched his car last night and found out Ray was the one who killed the guy he arrested me for, and that he did it because he was a client of Lisa's. He was jealous. We couldn't let him get away with it, Court."

She nodded.

"He would have come after the club again. Worse, after Lisa. We protect the girls at Polished. It's our job. He wouldn't have rested until he had her. Killin' someone over her was a clear indication."

"Okay," she whispered.

Okay?

What type of okay was that?

"The brothers want me to take you out to dinner for a tight alibi. They got him drunk and will organize a car crash with the evidence of his murder so the cops will find it and arrest him. The brothers and I... Shit, we beat him to make sure it looked like he got roughed up in the accident." Her gaze snapped from my shirt up to me when I'd said we'd beaten him. "I know it's hard to hear, especially since it's so fuckin' soon with us. Look, we don't have to go anywhere." I ran a hand over my head. "Fuck, I get it if this is too much. If you want to bail on this, us, I get—"

"Shut your mouth, Dominic Miller." She turned and went for her dress, leaving me wide-eyed and frozen. "I'll get dressed. You have a quick shower, and we can leave for dinner. But you're buying me ice cream for dessert."

"What?" I choked, struggling to comprehend what she was saying to me.

She faced me with her hands on her hips. "What? Did you think I wouldn't understand? Did you think I'd run? That *man* would have gotten away with murder. Like you said, he would have come at you, the club, and Lisa if he wasn't dealt with. Now it's being dealt with, and he won't interrupt our lives again." She gave me her back and threw off my tee to pull her dress on while ranting, "He's supposed to be a police officer. Someone who saves lives. Someone people can trust." She spun around and pointed at me. "No one can trust a person who does what he did because of a woman." Her finger moved toward the bathroom. "Go shower, Dom. People need to see you out and about."

Fuck me.

Fucking hell.

How'd I get so goddamn lucky?

"If I didn't have another man's blood on me, I'd kiss the hell out of you right now."

Her face softened. "I'd prefer not to get anything of him on me. I'll take you up on the kiss after."

"You got it, little mouse. But, baby, you've just gone and glued yourself to me, and you gotta know that even if I piss you off, you ain't gettin' rid of me."

She pressed a hand over her heart and said softly, "Dom."

Christ, I really wished I didn't have blood on me so I could show her how much I appreciated her support. There weren't many good ones out there who could accept the shit of our world and then get ready for dinner to give me an alibi.

Yeah, she was mine.

CHAPTER TWELVE

Courtney

After dinner, Dominic took me back to his place. A three-bedroom brick home in a quiet area. After walking me through his tidy house, he took me to bed and showed me just how much he appreciated how I'd handled things.

However, when I woke suddenly in the middle of the night and reached for him, I found I was alone. The sheet on his side was still a little warm, which told me he hadn't been gone long. Stretching, I flung back the blankets and sat on the side of the bed, blindly searching for the lamp on the bedside table. Once it was on, I picked up his tee and slipped it over my head. Scrubbing a hand over my face—thankfully I'd washed my makeup off already—I stood up and made my way out of the bedroom. We'd gone to bed with the bedroom door open, but it had since been closed.

Did he not want me to hear something?

Had someone come over?

I stopped in the hallway and wondered if I was supposed to go back to bed and wait for him. Scraping my top teeth over my bottom lip, I listened. There was a light on at the end of the hall where the kitchen was. But I didn't hear anyone speaking. Maybe he just got up and needed a drink. He could have had a nightmare about being in jail.

I knew if I'd had a nightmare, I would want comfort.

Nodding to myself, I made my way down the hall and into the kitchen. I paused in the doorway when I spotted Dominic leaning against the counter near the sink on the far side of the room. He stood wearing only black boxers, staring down at his phone in his hand.

"Dom?" I said gently.

His gaze rocked up and the soft smile he shared had tension rolling off my shoulders. Tension I hadn't known I'd been carrying.

"Everything okay?"

"Yeah, little mouse. What woke you?"

I shrugged. "I don't know. Maybe I felt you gone from the bed."

His gaze warmed. "Come here, baby." I did, and as soon as I was close, he put his phone on the counter, took my wrist, and tugged me forward where he could wrap his arms around me tight. I sighed into his chest, then kissed him there before I rested the side of my face against his warm skin.

"Words can't describe seein' you walk in here in my tee, little mouse. Knowin' you'd been in *my* bed. Knowin' only hours ago I was inside you."

A shiver raked over my body as my pussy clenched and nipples hardened. His words were a turn-on button I never knew I had. He knew it, he felt it, and when his fingers slid into my hair and pulled my head back, I gasped, then moaned when he kissed and nipped at my neck.

That was when he said softly, "And knowin' you're willin' to be here with me and becomin' mine."

"Dom," I whispered.

He straightened and pressed his lips against mine while I ran my hands up and down his chest. I definitely didn't miss the extra-hard bulge he now rocked against my stomach.

"You're addictive," he told me before biting at my bottom lip.

"So are you."

He pulled his head back. "Yeah?"

"Yes."

When his phone rang, his expression morphed into a serious one. "Shit. You're distracting too, little mouse." He curled an arm around my shoulders and tucked me into him. He picked up his phone. "Tech."

"You got your computer on?" I heard from the other end.

"Yeah, brother, like you told me. But one sec. Court just woke."

Tech's chuckle also traveled through the phone and then "Brother, it'd better be quick or you're gonna miss the fun," followed.

Dominic grunted and placed the phone down at his side. "Baby, Tech's got a live feed of Ray about to get taken down by cops who are on their way to where he is. It's why I'm up. Woke to Tech textin' me. You can either watch it or go back to bed and wait for me. I'm good with whatever you pick."

What did I want to do?

I knew he wouldn't be disappointed in me if I didn't want to watch.

But… I couldn't help feeling I wanted to see that prick being humiliated and taken in like he deserved.

He'd messed with Dom.

He'd killed.

He'd stalked.

Yes, I wanted to see his world crumble.

"I'd like to see the look in his eyes when he realizes his life is screwed."

His grin was big. "Fuck, you're perfect." He kissed me like he wasn't on a timeline. "My laptop's set up in the dinin' room." He grabbed his phone, took my hand, and led me toward the table. "Tech—" Dom laughed at something Tech said. "Yeah, brother, already know how lucky I am." He sat in the seat at the end of the table and pulled me down onto his lap. "All right, tell me what to do." While he played with the laptop, I swung my legs and sat sideways on his lap so I could wind my arm around his neck. Even as he talked on the phone, he kept glancing at me and giving me quick pecks to the temple, nose, cheek, and chin.

"You got it?" Tech asked.

"Yep."

I turned around, facing forward, and leaned into the table to get a closer look. Dom blanketed my back, brushing my hair over my shoulder. On the screen all we saw was shrubbery until whoever was filming pushed through enough so we could see the street.

Ray's car was destroyed, the driver's side smashed in from one of those industrial bins. The front had been driven into a roller door. Smoke billowed out from under the wrecked hood.

"Tech, who's there filmin'?"

Tech snorted. "Torch, who else. Even though he crashed the car and got a few scrapes and bruises, he wanted to stick around for the show. Wreck's there also, watching Torch and makin' sure Ray doesn't escape. Though he was pretty messed-up drunk at the end."

They quieted when we all heard sirens through the video. It didn't take long for the cops to show and the action to happen. They checked over the car and found Ray in the driver seat. Somehow, one of the cops managed to get the door open. We heard him cursing and taking a step back.

"Fucking hell, Ray. Did you shit yourself?"

Laughter sounded from the car along with some

gibberish words. The other cop was at the back of the car where the trunk was open a little. He pushed it the rest of the way and cursed.

"Bobby, call in more cars."

"What? Why? This is Ray. He's just drunk."

"There's bloody clothes and other shit in here. Call in backup now."

"Shit, fuck. Ray, what the hell have you done?"

Everything happened quickly after that. A team showed and went through the trunk while other officers questioned a very intoxicated Ray.

"Who did you hurt?"

Ray laughed. "Hurt? Me—they hurt me. But I killed him." More laughter from him as Dom and I shared a smile. He'd just screwed up his life without even knowing it. Whatever he would come up with now wouldn't stand in court because Torch wasn't the only one recording; another officer was, and he'd caught Ray's confession on camera.

Dom reached out and shut the laptop. He leaned back, dragging me against him with an arm around my waist. "Tech, talk soon."

Tech chuckled. "Yeah, yeah." The call ended.

"It's done," I said softly, smiling.

"It is. He won't get away with anythin' now."

Justice. "I'm glad, Dom."

"Me too, baby." His hand slipped up under his tee and rubbed over my stomach. "Like havin' you here in my house. Sharin' my life with you."

My body warmed and my pulse raced. "I like it too."

"Good. Get into bed, little mouse. Gonna shut things down and come fuck you."

"Okay," I breathed, my body tingling from his words.

I could definitely get used to this. Us.

CHAPTER THIRTEEN

Courtney

"You can back out at any time you like," I told Dominic for at least the tenth time, having just pulled up out the front of my parents' house for family dinner night.

"Woman, you ain't gettin' out of this. I'm lookin' forward to a home-cooked dinner."

I shot him a glare. "And what do you call all those dishes I made at your place, huh?"

Ever since the night Dom took me out to dinner for his alibi, we'd been inseparable. Usually, I would either get on a guy's nerves after twenty-four hours, or he would be on mine, and I'd need a break, but with Dominic, it was the opposite. Honestly, the way my feelings had grown for him in a week was new and exciting and scary all at the same time. Dominic and I had only spent one night apart from each other in the last week, and in that night alone, I didn't think I could miss a guy as much as I did him, yet it happened.

It was an extra hit to my emotions that he'd hadn't liked being apart either. He'd called me the next morning and told me to get my ass back to his place.

It would have been smarter to refuse since I was still a little worried it was happening too fast, but I hadn't. Couldn't.

I liked falling asleep beside him.

I liked waking up with him.

I liked how he got my coffee ready while I showered for work.

He enjoyed my company as much as I did his.

Bad days were bound to happen between us. Neither of us was perfect. We'd annoy each other eventually, probably argue, but I already believed we could work through whatever it was because we'd wanted the same outcome: a strong relationship.

Dominic grinned and cupped the back of my head, pulling me close. "A meal from *my* woman, which I fuckin' loved." He kissed me, and I was sure it was to shut me up. Not that I minded. "But you gotta know a mom's cookin' is always different."

Sighing, I had to agree. "Yes, that's true." I nodded. "Okay, let's do this."

"Babe," he called.

I turned to him before I got out. "Yes?"

"No matter what goes on, you gotta know you're stuck with me. You know I like what we've got goin' on, little mouse."

My body warmed. "I do, and I like it too, Dom."

He grunted. "Good."

When we met at the front of the car, he took my hand in his. I never thought he'd be a hand-holding type, but he always reached for mine when we were walking down the street or even sitting on the couch watching something.

I enjoyed how affectionate he was. Actually, I enjoyed a lot of things about him, but especially how the sex was out-of-this-world good.

At the door, Dom asked, "What're you thinkin' about?"

I turned into him, putting my arms around his waist. "Just how good you are in bed."

A throat cleared.

I hadn't even heard the door open.

Usually, no one waited and I just walked in.

But now, my three brothers stood in the doorway.

Casper screwed up his face. "I didn't need to know that."

Carter fake dry-retched, and Calvin closed the door in our faces.

Finding this hilarious, Dom chuckled. I smacked his stomach and opened the front door again. My brothers weren't in sight.

"She's out there now, telling the neighbors how good her guy is in bed," I heard Casper say.

"I am not!" I yelled, storming down the hallway and into the kitchen. "What were you freaks doing at the door anyway?"

"We just happened to be near it when you arrived," Calvin said from where he sat at the dining room table.

"Sweetheart," Mom called, "it's good to hear State pleases you in bed, but maybe it's best you don't tell everyone."

"I really didn't need to hear it," Dad added.

"That was a private conversation that these idiots weren't supposed to hear."

A hand landed on my shoulder.

Mom looked over my head. "State, it's great to see you."

"You too, Beth. Patty, thanks for havin' me for dinner."

"Let's just hope it's one of Beth's better meals," he joked and got a slap to the side from Mom.

"State, these are our boys. Carter, Calvin, and Casper. Boys, play nice."

When I glanced back at my brothers, they were all sitting on the opposite side of the table, glaring at Dom.

Groaning, I pointed at them. "Quit it."

"So," Carter drew out, "what are your intentions with our sister?"

Goddamn it.

Dom kissed my temple before moving over to the table, where he took a seat and leaned back. "She's mine. I'm hers. That's all you gotta know."

Carter opened his mouth, closed it, and looked at

Calvin, who steepled his hands and rested his chin on them. "Are you financially stable enough to provide for her?"

"State, ignore them," Mom tried.

I walked up, gripped the back of Dom's chair, and leaned into him. "They're only testing you because a... um, a guy I brought home a while back was intimidated by them and left."

Dom tipped his head back, and his jaw clenched. "Babe, it might be best you don't bring up anyone you've been on a date with, or I'll hunt them, find them, and kill them with the brothers at my back."

Casper clapped and stood. "Right, question time over." He leaned over the table and shook Dom's hand. "State, good to meet you, except for the fact that I think I shit myself."

"Casper," Mom cried. "Go to the bathroom."

Carter and then Calvin also shook his hand, seeming to accept him since he said he'd kill my exes.

"I have the address of a dickhead who I hated dating my sister. If you decide to kill him, can I come watch?" Carter asked.

"Sure," Dom said with a smirk.

"Dom, hon, no taking my brothers to any killings."

"We'll talk later," Carter said.

"State, a word please," Dad called.

I tensed until Dom stood up, tipped up my chin, and ran his gaze over my face. "It's all good, little mouse."

"I know."

Then he proceeded to kiss me in front of everyone.

And I didn't mean a quick peck. No. When Dominic kissed, he put everything into it.

He owned me.

Possessed me.

And I loved every heated touch.

Then he walked out of the room, leaving me red-faced and breathing heavily.

"Why do I have the urge to slap your back and say congratulations?" Casper asked.

"I need to bleach my eyes," Carter grumbled.

Calvin sighed. "I threw up a bit in my mouth all while second-guessing my sexuality."

"Shut up, boys," Mom scolded. "Sweetheart, anyone with eyes can see how he looks at you."

Turning to her, I asked, "How?"

"Like you're his world."

A tingle spread through my belly. Yet I shook my head, still not quite believing any of this was real. Meeting someone who ticked every box I looked for in a guy, plus about fifty more I'd never even considered before Dominic, never happened to me. "Don't get your hopes up, Mom. It's still early days, and he could get sick of me." I winced at my own words. I seriously had to stop belittling myself and letting my past relationships rule my thoughts like I told Dominic I would.

I had to remind myself I *was* worth the time of day.

I *did* deserve Dominic.

I *was* pretty. I was sexy.

My confidence would take time, but I would get there.

My brothers snorted in unison. It was freaky when they did things like that.

"What?"

"Nothing," Carter said, shaking his head.

"No… what?" I took the seat opposite them.

But they only shared a look and kept their mouths closed. Of course, I kicked the closest one under the table.

Calvin cursed. Mom scolded.

"We've only just met him and already know he's into you. Deep into you."

"Dude," Casper yelled with his nose screwed up.

Calvin blanched. "I didn't mean it like that, you dick."

"Boys, enough. Dinner's ready. Come help me take it to the table." Their chairs scraped along the floor when they stood up and did as Mom asked. All the while, I thought over what they'd said.

Yes, Dominic did say he saw a future between us, and I hoped that was the truth, because, well, I wanted to claim him as mine. Maybe I needed to put more effort into actually believing him and believing my brothers when they told me stuff like how deeply Dominic felt for me.

Despite it being such a short amount of time.

My brothers placed the platters on the table, and I jolted from hands on my shoulders. Dom's scent filled my senses when he leaned down and whispered, "You good?"

Tipping my head to the side, I smiled. "Yes. You?"

"Yeah, baby. Just talkin' about the shit that went down." He took the seat next to me as Mom told us to dig in. Dom picked up my plate and started to pile it with a bit of everything. He didn't notice everyone who watched him. He didn't notice the soft smile on my parents' faces or when Calvin mouthed, "I told you."

Dominic placed my food in front of me, hooked a hand to the back of my head, and drew me in for a kiss. "Eat, little mouse," he ordered before he helped himself to food.

That was it.

I was going to kidnap this man forever.

LATER, when we walked into Dominic's home, he shut the door behind him, took my hand, and spun me back around to face him.

"You've been quiet. What's wrong?"

Smiling, I shook my head. "Nothing." Except I couldn't stop seeing the little things he'd do for me, and each time I did, my heart grew and grew for this man in front of me.

How could I feel so much so soon?

It didn't make sense, yet I couldn't seem to care. I wanted to feel this way about him because he was special.

"That's bull, Court. Did I do somethin'?"

How could he think that? My parents loved him. My brothers were infatuated with him and his stories. Of course they begged to be invited to the clubhouse. Who wouldn't love him when Dominic could easily have you relaxed and happy around him?

He was smooth, smart, hot, and amazed me every day we spent time together. I also loved his strong belief in protection over his family.

Lifting onto my toes, I wrapped my arms around his neck. "You couldn't do anything wrong."

He smirked. "Don't count on that, babe. You were yellin' at me last week about me leavin' my towel on the floor."

Smiling, I rolled my eyes. "Okay, you have some flaws, but I think you're something special."

His arms convulsed around me. "Yeah?"

"Yes. And maybe that's why I've been quiet. I don't know if feeling this connected to you is a good thing or bad because it's so soon, but now I don't care. If you try to run, I'll kidnap you."

His laugh was loud and happy. When it slowed, he dipped to kiss my neck. "I might run just to see how this kidnappin' plan goes."

"I have a feeling your brothers will help me out."

He grunted, amused. "They would, the traitors. Though, I wouldn't fight them too much because I like bein' around you."

He made me smile.

He made me giddy.

He made me light.

There was just so much I felt for him. I didn't want to call it love yet, but it was close to it.

"If you like me, does that mean you're going to take me to bed?"

His brow rose. "I have a better idea."

"What's that?"

"Take your panties off, sit on the couch, and spread your legs."

A thrill swept through me, and I shivered. "Dom."

"Now, little mouse," he demanded in a deeper, darker tone.

My nipples hardened, and my breath caught. Licking my suddenly dry lips, I walked over to the couch, glancing over my shoulder to see Dom was where I left him, leaning against the door. I slipped my panties down and kicked them off with my heels.

I tucked my dress under my butt and sat on the couch, spreading my legs. I heard his approach, then felt his hand slide into my hair before he tugged my head back. Our eyes connected.

"Good girl," he clipped.

My breaths panted out of me as I watched him removing his club vest and tee. The vest went over the back of the couch, the tee to the floor.

He dropped to his knees and slowly lifted the front of my dress.

"Scoot forward, baby. I'm gonna need to eat and make a mess."

Another tingle spread through me, and my heart raced when I moved my ass to the edge of the couch. He clasped me under my thighs and opened me further, dipping in and kissing the top of my mound before dragging his tongue down my slit.

He started slowly before tightening his hold on me and devouring me with licks, sips, and nips. I threaded my fingers through his hair and held on, moaning and crying out his name.

My legs tightened around his head, but he pried them open to push two fingers inside me.

"Dom, God, please, so close."

He sucked and licked at my clit while fingering me fast. I gasped and whimpered.

"Come for me, little mouse," he ordered, and tongued my clit. I gasped, eyes wide, body tightening, and did as he asked.

He lifted himself over me with his pants already undone and rolled the condom on. Where he got it from, I didn't know, didn't care, and then he was deep inside me. My walls clenched around him, and I wrapped him up, arms and legs surrounding him while he fucked me hard and fast, kissing my neck. Driving me wild and edging me closer to another orgasm.

"Fuck, baby. Fuck, little mouse. You feel so good. Goddamn."

"Love you in me, Dom. Love the feel of you."

"Yeah, baby. Fuck, yes." He kissed me, and I sucked on his tongue as he drilled into me, bringing me closer and closer.

I broke the kiss to whimper his name as my body ignited, climax overtaking me.

Coming down, Dom pulled out of me and stood up,

cupping the back of my head in one hand and removing the condom with the other. "Taste me, baby. Drink me down."

I dove onto his cock, licking, sucking, and then drinking when he shot his load into my mouth with a deep, grunted groan. He removed his cock and instantly moved me without warning. I squealed until he was lying over me, kissing me deep and soft.

Dominic Miller definitely made me feel so much, and I couldn't wait to see where it led us in the future.

EPILOGUE

(Six months after Country's book.)

State

I walked in the front door and heard nothing but silence. An invisible fist clenched around my heart, and I threw my keys onto the table near the door where my wife argued we needed to keep them and bolted into the living room.

Taking a deep breath, I rubbed at my chest and stared at my family asleep on the couch.

My wife.

My son.

Fuck.

My shit mood over what Death had discovered

disappeared. It flew out the fucking window because I got to come home to this. My family. *Mine.*

I grinned when I noted Crispin was leaving a pile of drool on Court's chest. I made my way over and picked up my son, cradling him in my arms.

I glanced back down at my little mouse and saw her eyes were open and looking at me with a soft stare.

"He's been grumpy all day from a temperature."

I tipped my chin up at her. "I've got him, baby. Go grab a shower or get some more rest. I'll see if he'll go down."

She blinked tiredly up at me. "You're the best."

Winking, I took our boy to his room. She was wrong. I wasn't the best because that title went to her. My life changed when she walked into it, and only for the better. Yeah, we'd had our moments of arguing over bullshit things; it happened to everyone, and we got over it eventually, because no matter what it was about, it wasn't worth losing sleep over… or her.

I lay Crispin in his little bed, and he stirred a bit but went back to sleep. He'd been such a good baby. Never whined without reason.

I wanted another.

Loved when Court was knocked up with my kid. She looked goddamn amazing with her round belly. Christ, just thinking of it had my grin growing.

Could I talk her into another so soon?

Crispin was nearly two.

I'd never forget the day she'd found out she was pregnant. Turned out the condom I'd used in the shower the very first time had broken. A sudden wave of pride had me puffing out my chest. I chuckled low when I thought of the moment when Courtney realized.

We'd been at the compound with her brothers a couple months after being together, sitting around a table. Well, most of us had been.

"Country'll kick Casper's ass," I commented, tugging *Courtney, who was sitting on my lap, closer to my chest. Court, Carter, and Calvin glanced over at their brother who stood at the bar talking to Dusty.*

Death chuckled from where he sat at the table.

"Why?" Carter asked.

"Doesn't matter why, but it might be best to go save him," I told them and then thought of the best way to distract Casper from Dusty. "Stracy," I called, and the club girl swayed her hips over toward us with a smile. She placed one hand on Carter's shoulder and the other on Calvin's. "Hey, what's up?"

"The guy at the bar talkin' to Dusty. Can you get his attention and lead him back over here?"

She took a long look at Casper and smiled. "I don't mind at all."

We all watched her work her magic when she got to him. Dusty shot Stracy a smile and slipped off her stool to make her way into the kitchen. I didn't mind that Stracy stayed at the bar a while longer talking with Casper now that Dusty was out of the picture and Country wasn't staring daggers at my woman's brother.

Torch appeared at the table. He bounced on his feet a

couple of times, flipped a chair around, and straddled it while looking at Carter.

"You're him, right?"

Carter smiled. "Depends who 'him' is."

"You're on the Wolves team."

"Yeah, that's me."

"I told you, fuckers," Torch yelled across the room before he up and left again.

Shock had my brows shooting high. "You play?"

"I do."

"How'd I not know this?" I commented. "What about you?" I asked Calvin.

"Sports isn't my thing. I'm studying to become a defense attorney in family law."

"That's a good job," I said, and Calvin shrugged. "What about Casper?"

The siblings shared a look. Courtney shifted on my lap and told me, "He's in between jobs at the moment, but he'd like to get into acting."

"Good-lookin' kid, I'm sure he'd get somethin'," Death said just as Stracy and Casper arrived back at the table.

Stracy had Casper sit down while he looked up at her with stars in his eyes. Stracy winked. "I'll come find you soon."

He grinned. "Looking forward to it." His gaze stayed glued to her ass as she walked away. He whistled low. "You guys must go through a ton of condoms."

Chuckling, I shrugged and received a death stare from Courtney. I cupped the side of her face and kissed her soundly. Against her lips, I said, "Never had a taste for club pussy, little mouse. And now you're the only one I want and need."

She drew in a slow, shaky breath. "Good answer."

She turned back to the table and leaned forward for a drink just as Casper said, "And tampons, if they all live here."

I felt her still on my lap. I ignored what they were talking about and ran my hand up her back. "You good, little mouse?"

She stood up, her eyes wide as she backed up a step.

Worry seared into my gut. "Court?" I straightened up out of the chair.

"I... I don't know how.... I'm sorry."

"Sorry? For what?"

She got close and leaned into me as she went onto her tiptoes and whispered into my ear, "I haven't got my period, Dom."

I turned to stone, and she went back down onto her feet, looking up at me, worrying her bottom lip with her teeth.

My heart doubled its beat as I looked down at her stomach.

She was carrying my baby.

I didn't know how since we'd used rubbers, but fuck, it was meant to be.

All along we were always meant to be.

I was going to be a father.

Lifting my gaze to her face, I realized I'd taken too long for it to sink in. Tears filled her eyes, her shoulder slumping as she took another step back.

"Courtney, what's going on?" Carter demanded hard, and the room quieted.

My hand shot out to shut him up. I kept my eyes on Courtney. "I told you."

Her head jerked back. "What?" she whispered.

"I told you, little mouse, that we were meant to be. Been holding off sayin' it, and I'm gonna get into shit from the brothers for doin' it here, but you gotta know, baby, you're mine. I fuckin' love you."

A sob caught in her throat as her tears fell, and she pressed her hands to her belly.

"Carter, call Beth and tell her she's gonna get grandkids sooner than she thought."

"What?" I was sure all three brothers yelled.

"Dom, you can't tell her yet. I need to make sure first."

"I've got a test," one of the girls called, and she ran off for it.

"Baby, come here."

"Dom, this isn't—"

"Court, come here."

She sighed and stepped right in front of me. I tipped her chin up to me. "You want my kid?"

"It's so soon," she whispered.

"Didn't ask that, little mouse. If it happens you are pregnant, will you be happy?"

"Will you?" I could see she was more scared about what I thought than what she thought herself.

"Thought I couldn't get any happier with you in my life. Found out moments ago that I could."

She swallowed thickly and nodded, pressing herself close. "I love you too, and yes, I will be happy if I am."

With the test in hand, Courtney went to the bathroom. I'd

never seen the brothers hang around like hovering flies until then as we waited close by for an answer. When Courtney walked out of the bathroom with new tears in her eyes and a smile, the room erupted in cheers.

I walked up to my woman, picked her up in my arms, and kissed the fuck out of her for making me so fucking ecstatic. My body hummed from it.

Thinking back on it, I knew that night I was going to put my ring on her finger and make sure every prick knew she was taken. She was mine.

Walking through the house, I found my woman not resting, not in the shower or the bath, but in the kitchen doing the dishes.

I wrapped my arms around her from behind. "Leave them, little mouse. I'll grab them later."

"It's okay. It won't take long."

"Babe" was all I said, which had her laughing.

"It's fine. Guess who called today?"

"Who?"

"Isla."

I tensed. "You're fuckin' with me? What'd that bitch want?" She'd been cheating on Country back in the day, and he'd found out it was with a guy from another club. A club we hated. He'd been the one supplying her with drugs.

"How sorry she is and that she's met someone who makes her happy. He sounds good for her. She actually sounded genuine. She wants to meet up one day. Knows I'm with you, that I should check with you before I say yes."

"Do you want to?"

"Honestly, I don't know. Maybe, just to rub in her face how happy I am. How good Country is doing now he's with Dusty. Does that sound bad? Petty?"

"Doesn't matter how it sounds. You do what you wanna do, baby. But I'm comin' with you."

"You don't trust her?"

"No."

"The guy she's with is a banker. He sounds boring."

Chuckling, I kissed her neck. "Good. She probably needs it."

"She does." She turned in my arms and ran her hands up my chest. "I should really thank her for taking me along that night and giving me the man of my dreams."

"Yeah?"

She looked up at me with heat in her eyes. "If it wasn't for her, I wouldn't be where I am now."

"True."

"Dom?"

"Yeah, little mouse."

"We have about an hour before Crispin's awake. Do you think you could make me come in that time?"

I picked her up, sat her ass on the counter, and rocked into her. "I reckon I could." I removed her tee and bra, cupped her tits, and sucked a nipple into my mouth. "What would you say if I said I'd love to see you with my baby in here again?" I rubbed across her stomach.

Her breath hitched. "That I better go off the pill then."

My grin was damn big as I lifted my head. "You want another?"

"Yes." She nodded. I grabbed my phone out of my pocket and was ready to hit dial when Court stole it from me. "What are you doing?"

"Callin' your mom to let her know she'll have another grandkid comin'."

Laughing, she shook her head. "How about we wait until it actually happens?"

When I picked her up, she wrapped her legs around me. "Then let's get down to business."

"Okay," she said against my throat, where she nipped.

Sex was beyond damn good with my little mouse, but our lives weren't just about that. She made me happy. She completed me in ways I didn't know I was missing until she'd filled them.

My life couldn't be more perfect than it was with my woman, my old lady, my wife.

READ ON FOR A LOOK INSIDE
WRECK'S STORY:

Wreck me Forever is book #1 in the
Polished P & P series.

Lucas

Groaning, I brushed my free hand through my shoulder-length blond curls and then tapped my phone against my forehead. Why did my brother have to have his biker friends over tonight?

Yes, it was his house.

Yes, he could do what he wanted in it.

To some extent.

I could have gone without seeing him drilling one of his flings over the kitchen table. A table where I would always make sure to sit at the opposite end after witnessing that scene.

It was just that I'd had a shit day. One of the worst.

I'd woken late because I'd forgotten to set the alarm. It had rained, which caused me to get drenched, and then I'd slipped as I walked into class, landing on my ass. I was sure it would be bruised by tomorrow. Of course, everyone had a good chuckle over it. Lastly, I nearly got run over on the way home. The stupid dick didn't want to give way to a pedestrian and decided my life was fair game.

It was lucky I moved out of the way fast enough. Though, as I did, I got a good look at the driver. Mitch dickface Henry. He and I had gone to the same high school, and I'd hoped to be rid of him through college, but I wasn't. He had it out for me, always had, ever since it was proven that I excelled in class. He wanted to be the best, but there I was tarnishing his perfect grades with my better ones. It wasn't like I meant it. I just loved learning.

I could still hear his taunting laugh.

When would the dweeb grow up?

With a shake of my head, I finished my walk down the street to my brother's place. It was two months ago when our parents moved from Nevada to Australia, and sold their place, to see if it suited them in retirement. So, Zion, my brother, offered up his spare room so I could stay and finish the fourth year of my pre-med degree, then med school before I found a placement and started my residency training at a hospital.

I'd been surprised he'd offered it to me. Zion was five years older than me, and we were so different from each other, it was funny. I was the nerd, the quiet guy who was clumsy, spoke before he thought—or stumbled over his words—and was uncomfortable in crowded rooms. Zion was the life of the party. Popular and fun-loving, he didn't care what anyone thought. Unfortunately, I did, but I was slowly learning not to.

What helped when Zion offered his place was that we both knew we would be busy and hardly be in each other's space since I liked a place where I could study in peace. Which I did a lot. When I wasn't in class, I had my head buried in a book. I had a job at the local café, which also contained an electronics store where I helped out with repairs on gaming systems. Zion was busy with the business he'd gone into with some of his friends.

Our parents were proud of him, especially since Polished Pussy was doing so well. Even if it was a brothel, our parents didn't care as long as Zion was happy in what he was doing. Mom had wanted a tour of the place, but when Zion said it was open day and night and that he wouldn't feel comfortable taking her through a place where people had sex, she'd glared and asked, "How do you think you and your brother were made?"

I quickly ran from the room before I heard any more, but Mom got her tour and had come home gloating about how she knew it would expand because of how clean it was and how sweet the ladies were. No doubt she would have sat down and found out about the working girls' lives while sipping tea and probably commenting on their skills.

I shuddered at the thought. However, Mom was right. Zion and his friends were opening another two Polished Pussies in the neighboring cities in the next month.

Heck, I was even proud of my brother. I never thought a brothel with the name Polished Pussy would take off.

I'd been wrong.

When I'd asked him about the name, he'd snorted and said, "We'd been throwing names around all night, but then, after a few joints, someone said they'd like to polish their woman's pussy with their tongue. We all looked at each other and yelled, 'Polished Pussy.' It stuck, and thank fuck it worked."

I wish I hadn't asked. I didn't need to know about his friend wanting to… do *that* to a woman.

You see, my brother didn't know I wouldn't want to talk about women and their body parts. He didn't know that it didn't interest me, because he didn't know I was gay.

Our parents didn't even know.

Why I hadn't told anyone, I didn't have a clue. I knew they would support me, but every time I went to open my mouth to inform them I liked dick, I felt it wasn't the right moment. Instead, time passed, and I kept my mouth shut. In the end, they moved without the knowledge, and I shifted into my brother's home. My brother, who was the straightest guy I knew. I wasn't even sure about his stance on gay people, which was another reason I hadn't said anything.

I couldn't exactly say, "Ah, hey, bro, what do you think about guys getting it on?" No matter how I said it, I knew it would come out wrong, then I would freak out if I thought he was going to be disgusted.

Now, I had to go into his house full of his friends, who I hadn't met before, and pray I didn't check any of them out too long. Sighing, I closed my eyes and rested my head against the front door. Already I could hear the voices of Zion and his friends. They had music playing in the background, but what it was, I didn't have a clue.

Straightening, I brushed my hands down my NASA tee and then reached out to the handle. Before I could grab hold, the door got swept open, and I stumbled forward so hard my head collided with a crotch. As I landed on my hands and knees, my head slipped down further and rested against someone's muscled thighs.

The only problem with Zion's house was the open-floor living.

Laughter filled the area.

"Brothers, I'd like you to meet my younger, and clumsy, brother, Lucas."

A hand under my arm helped me. Actually, it practically lifted me on its own to my feet. "You okay, kid?" the large man asked.

"Yes," I squeaked. I cleared my throat and punched my chest, then lowered my voice. "Ah, yeah, I'm good."

The man smiled. His perfect white teeth between his trimmed beard captured my attention. He seemed in his mid-forties, but he looked good for it. His salt-and-pepper hair was styled back in a ponytail. He nodded. "Good. Sorry about the abrupt open. Thought you were some crazy fucker staking out the joint or the pizza guy."

I nodded. And kept nodding since I didn't know what to say.

"Name's Death." He held his tattooed hand out that was attached to his tattooed arm. I noticed his other arm was also inked.

Nervously, I licked my lips and stared at the large appendage—meaning his hand—that was still outstretched toward me. His name sounded like he would use his hands to kill people. I was too young and small, well, compared to him, and nice to die. Still, even when my hand shook, I pushed it forward and gripped his. "Lucas," I said.

Death snorted. "Already heard."

I wanted to slap my forehead. "Yeah, right." I forced a laugh.

Using my hand, he pulled me further into the room, then he dropped his hold and pointed to another huge guy. "That's Quake, Torch, and the prospect. He doesn't get a club name until he's a full member." I nodded to them all. Quake was a solid man, heck, all of them were, but he was the biggest. His hair was blond and messy, and it went perfectly with his sea-blue eyes. Torch had a buzz cut and a cold look in his eyes where I worried if I looked too long, I would ask for forgiveness even when I hadn't done anything. The prospect was the youngest. Where I was twenty-two, he seemed to be in his early twenties also, but it was hard to determine just what his age actually was.

The front door opened abruptly behind me. I bit my bottom lip to keep in the scream. But that didn't stop me from jumping and stumbling as I turned, and if it wasn't for Death's hand wrapping around my arm, I would have met the floor once more that night.

However, when I looked up, I realized there was still a possibility of dropping to the floor. The most gorgeous man I had ever seen stood just inside the doorway, scanning the room. If it wasn't for his hands fisted at his sides and the scowl on his face, I may have fallen to the floor in awe of his beauty.

I took another quick glance around the room and noticed my brother did, in fact, have some good-looking friends. All of them could be on the cover of a magazine. I wasn't sure what it was about the scowling man that set me off in a sweating, peeing-my-pants, "holy crap he's looking at me" moment with my pulse racing, but he did. His dark brown hair was shaved at the sides, and the top was longish and messy, some of it flopped in his dark green eyes. He would probably punch me if I tried to push his hair back though. He was tall, my short frame only reaching his shoulders. His tight black tee showed off the muscles in his arms, and his dark ripped jeans surrounded thick thighs.

I jolted and pulled my gaze up quickly when Death said, "Wreck, you took forever, fucker. Get in here and meet Saint's brother, Lucas."

Saint?

Who was Saint?

I wasn't a brother of Saint.

"Lucas, I'm Saint. It's my club name," Zion called; he must have seen the confused look on my face.

Nodding, I glanced back to Wreck and did a lame wave before I grabbed my own arm with my other hand. "Ah, s'up."

S'up?

Was I a gangster now?

"I mean, hi."

He lifted his chin, and out of his mouth came a gravelly, "Hey." He looked at Death. "Pizza guy just pulled up." Then he walked by us and aimed for the kitchen.

I wanted to follow like a stray kitten. He could take me in, pat me, love me…. Dear God, I'd finally lost it over a good-looking *straight* guy.

A slap to my back had me clamping my lips together and eyes widening. "Fuckin' pizza, gotta love that shit," Death said before he moved toward the still-open front door.

I heard a greeting before my arm was snagged, and Zion dragged me from the room, down the hall toward my bedroom. Had I done something already?

In my room, Zion closed the door and turned to me. "Are you okay with this? We've been on a long road trip and were close by, so instead of heading back to the compound, we stopped here for some food and drinks."

I waved a hand around. "It's fine." I laughed. "Totally fine. I mean, it's your place. You can do whatever."

His eyes narrowed as he crossed his arms over his chest. "Are you okay?"

"Yep," I popped and nodded. I threw an arm out. "I mean, I know you've been with your group—"

"Club. The Diamond MC," Zion stated with a smirk.

"Right, the MC club for a while. I just thought that if I ever met your guys—"

"Brothers." He chuckled.

"Yep, um, brothers, that they'd find me, ah, not cool."

Zion snorted. "Is this you being worried about what they'll think of you because you're gay?"

My heart stopped, my breath caught, and I wheezed, "You know?"

Zion smiled. "Shit, Lucas. Mom, Dad, and I know. We've known for years now."

I felt sick to the stomach. "How?"

"Besides the fact you look at guys before women?" he asked. I glared and nodded. He grinned. "Mom found some gay porn on your laptop one day when she went to use it."

I didn't have to see to know I'd paled. I *felt* the color drain from my face.

I sat on my bed with my head in my hands. "That's just so wrong on so many levels." I looked up. "I won't be able to face her. I'll have to leave the family."

Zion laughed, and I wanted to punch him. Heck, I'd never been a violent guy, but I was suddenly seeing the appeal of smashing someone's face in.

"Relax, I'm messing with you. It was me who found

the porn, but I'd already suspected. Mom just asked me one day if you'd said anything to me about liking guys."

I dropped back on the bed and covered my face. "Obviously I'm terrible at hiding it."

"Bro, we're family. We're gonna notice more than anyone. None of my high school friends suspected. What I don't get, though, is why you haven't told us?"

I groaned. "Is now really the time to have this talk when you have friends out there?"

"Yeah, it is." He moved over to my bed and sat next to me. When I didn't move, he shoved my leg. "Seriously, bro. Why didn't you say anything?"

I shrugged. "I don't know. I just got used to keeping it quiet."

"You know we don't care, right? You're you, no matter who you want between your sheets."

"Zion," I groaned, heat hitting my face.

"It's true."

Sighing, I finally sat back up. "I kind of knew you, Mom, and Dad would be okay with it. But even though it seems more accepted this day and age, Zion, it doesn't make it easier to come out. There's still haters."

"Some people just need to be taught a lesson. If anyone fucks with you, Lucas, you tell me."

Rolling my eyes, I gave him a small smile. "I can take care of myself. When I'm ready, I'll tell whoever I want I'm gay, but I want to be comfortable within myself first. I've only… had one, um, you know, experience…." I rubbed the back of my neck. "But I haven't… there hasn't been anyone special in my life to date."

"I get it. Just as long as you know I have your back. Mom and Dad will as well. But also, my brothers won't be like any of those bigoted fuckers," he stated. "Hell, if they are, they'll deal with me."

I bumped his shoulder again. "You're an okay kind of brother, Zion."

He snorted. "Just okay? I'm the best. Now, you gonna come out there and have some pizza?"

"Give me a minute, and I will."

His hand slapped down on my shoulder and squeezed. "You got it." I watched him walk from my room, and in a way, it felt like a small weight had been lifted off my shoulders. I should have guessed my family would have known I was gay even before telling them. They did know me the best. Even if Zion traveled in different circles to me, he'd always made sure he was there for me if needed. I just never asked.

I'd promised myself when I moved out of the family home and into Zion's that I would start living and being who I really wanted to be.

I guessed it was time to begin.

Glancing to the closed door, I heard deep laughter down the hall. There were *bikers* out there. Bikers I didn't know. However, they did seem like okay guys, and I knew my brother wouldn't be a part of their group... club if they weren't, but could they honestly accept me?

I wasn't sure, and that was damn scary.

Still, it was worth a try. It was probably time I did come out of my shell. I hadn't had many friends in high school. Those I had had gone off to different colleges. Those who stuck around made new friends, and we'd drifted apart. Though, I was lucky enough to have a couple of friends from college where we got together every now and then to catch up and wind down from studies.

So, it could be good to go out there and make new friends.

Another roar of laughter filled the house.

Then again, friends were overrated.

LILA ROSE

POLISHED P&P
SERIES

Wreck Me
FOREVER

Hawks MC: next generation

Coyote

Ruin (m/m)

Coming soon: Texas

Polished P & P series (m/m romance)

Wreck Me Forever

Never a Saint

Working Out West

Diamond MC

Country

State (novella)

Coming in 2023: Death

Romantic Comedies

Making Changes

Making Sense

***

Fumbled Love

Bumbled Love

Trinity Love Series

Left to Chance (m/m/f novel)

Love of Liberty (m/m/f novella)

Standalones

In The Dark (paranormal)

Havoc's Mate (paranormal novella)

Senseless Attraction (Y/A)

<u>**Titles under L. Rose**</u>

The Hidden Kingdom Trilogy

(reverse harem romance)

A Torn Paige

A Lost Paige

A Final Paige

Standalones

Infinite Bond (paranormal harem m/m/m/m)

www.ingramcontent.com/pod-product-compliance
Lightning Source LLC
Chambersburg PA
CBHW060931050726
47592CB00003B/905